LITTLE PINK BOOK
▬▬▬▬▬▬

OLIVIA KAN-SPERLING

小粉红书
▬▬▬▬▬▬

甘英

TRANSLATED BY CHEN S.

陈诗译

© 2025 Olivia Kan-Sperling

Endpapers from Diane Severin Nguyen's
In Her Time (Iris's Version), 2024.

All rights reserved. No part of this book may be reproduced in any manner in any media, or transmitted by any means whatsoever, electronic or mechanical (including photocopy, film or video recording, internet posting, or any other information storage and retrieval system), without the prior written permission of the publisher.

Published in the United States by:
Archway Editions,
a division of powerHouse Cultural Entertainment, Inc.
32 Adams Street, Brooklyn, NY 11201

www.archwayeditions.us

Daniel Power, CEO
Chris Molnar, Editorial Director
Nicodemus Nicoludis, Managing Editor
Naomi Falk, Senior Editor
Mia Risher, Publicist

Edited by Naomi Falk and Chris Molnar
Chinese translation by Chen S.
Proofread by Nanfu Wang

Library of Congress Control Number: 2024949893

ISBN 978-1-64823-041-7

Printed by Toppan Leefung

First edition, 2025

10 9 8 7 6 5 4 3 2 1

Printed and bound in China

EDITIONS

LITTLE PINK BOOK

OLIVIA KAN-SPERLING

ARCHWAY EDITIONS / BROOKLYN / NY

目录

~ 第一句孔子箴言 ~
序章: 他点燃了我, 像一根火柴

第一部分: 浪漫、敏感、艺术气息

~ 法国电影箴言 ~
第一章: 生活什么时候才能找到我?
第二章: 笔记本摄像头与可爱的拼贴画
第三章: 桃色夜晚
第四章: 甜梦造型
第五章: 秘密梦境造型
第六章: 黎美的秘密梦境生活
第七章: 再一次, 再一次, 再一次 (我想感受你的车灯照在我的脸上)

第二部分: 用力过猛

~ 第二句孔子箴言 ~
第八章: 一件充满图案的T恤
第九章: 粗鲁的男孩
第十章: 淋浴场景
第十一章: 一个出乎意料的问题
第十二章: 一场告白
第十三章: 不打破几颗蛋就做不成蛋饼…
第十四章: 一个孕育的停 (意味深长的停顿)
第十五章: 东方明珠的午餐
第十六章: 纯如粉色牛奶

第三部分: 歇斯底里的魅力

~ 李小龙箴言 ~
第十七章: 昏厥沙发 (躺椅)
第十八章: 色戒——别跌倒!
第十九章: 情感戏剧

TABLE OF CONTENTS

~ First Confucian Proverb ~
Prologue: He Lit Me Like a Match

PART 1: ROMANTIC, SENSITIVE, ARTISTIC

~ French Film Proverb ~
Chapter 1: When Will Life Ever Find Me?
Chapter 2: Laptop Camera and Cute Collage
Chapter 3: Peach Skin Nights
Chapter 4: Sweet Dreams Outfit
Chapter 5: Secret Dreams Outfit
Chapter 6: Limei's Secret Dream Life
Chapter 7: Again, Again, Again (I Want to Feel Your Headlights on My Face)

PART 2: HEAVY-HANDED

~ Second Confucian Proverb ~
Chapter 8: A Very Graphic T-Shirt
Chapter 9: Rude Boy
Chapter 10: Shower Scene
Chapter 11: A Surprising Question
Chapter 12: A Confession
Chapter 13: You Have to Break a Few Eggs…
Chapter 14: A Pregnant Pause
Chapter 15: Lunch at the Oriental Pearl
Chapter 16: Pure as Pink Milk

PART 3: HYSTERIC GLAMOUR

~ Bruce Lee Proverb ~
Chapter 17: Fainting Couch
Chapter 18: Lust, Caution—Don't Fall!
Chapter 19: Melodrama

第二十章: 针灸
第二十一章: 最残酷的评论
第二十二章: 原声带
第二十三章: 她的最后一杯拿铁
第二十四章: 迷失在深渊中

第四部分: 乖女孩变坏

~ 第三句孔子箴言 ~
第二十五章: 无牵牵无挂
第二十六章: 鸽子的初次飞翔
第二十七章: 完美蓝
第二十八章: 红晕反应
第二十九章: 珍珠牡丹
第三十章: 蒙太奇
第三十一章: 电视特别节目
第三十二章: 炒蛋
第三十三章: 沉默的星星
第三十四章: 对话
第三十五章: 神风特攻
第三十六章: "救命, 我怀孕了"

尾声: 再一次, 再一次, 再一次

~ 第四句孔子箴言 ~
第三十七章: 来自北京的电话
鸡第三十八章: 或蛋？（田园景色）
未完待续……

注
延伸阅读

Chapter 20: Acupuncture
Chapter 21: The Cruelest Comments
Chapter 22: Soundtrack
Chapter 23: Her Last Latte
Chapter 24: Mise en Abîme

PART 4: GOOD GIRL GONE BAD

~ *Third Confucian Proverb* ~
Chapter 25: No Strings Attached
Chapter 26: Dove's First Flight
Chapter 27: Perfect Blue
Chapter 28: Blush Response
Chapter 29: Pearl Peony
Chapter 30: Montage
Chapter 31: TV Special
Chapter 32: Scrambled Eggs
Chapter 33: Silent Star
Chapter 34: Dialogue
Chapter 35: Kamikaze
Chapter 36: "Help, I'm Pregnant"

EPILOGUE: AGAIN, AGAIN, AGAIN

~ *Fourth Confucian Proverb* ~
Chapter 37: A Call From Beijing
Chapter 38: Chicken or Egg? (Pastoral Scene)
To Be Continued...

Note
Further Reading

~ First Confucian Proverb ~

"In the Book of Poetry there are three hundred poems, but the meaning of all of them may be put in a single sentence: Have no debasing thoughts."

—Confucius

~ 第一句孔子箴言 ~

*"《诗经》三百篇，
其义一言以蔽之：思无邪。"*

—孔子

序章: 他点燃了我, 像一根火柴

序章: 他点燃了我, 像一根火柴
别这样!"女孩咯咯笑着,扭动着肩膀躲开。"你不想回去跳舞吗?"

"我喜欢待在这里。" 他耸了耸肩。

她听到一声轻微的嘶响,接着看见火柴的火光。她的眼睛跟随着他手中的香烟,随着它在手指间的移动发出微弱的光芒。屋顶在她眼前铺展开来,粗糙的混凝土、陡峭的边缘、无尽闪烁的城市。下面的车流川流不息,但这里的空气却是黑暗而静止的。一种刺痛的感觉袭来,像灯光洒落在拥挤剧场的瞬间……

"好吧,我想我还是……"

是的,她回想起小时候,在熙攘的剧院里,灯光逐渐熄灭。她向旁边挪了一步。但就在那时,他的手紧紧抓住了她的臀部。

"嘿,别走。" 他随意地说道。

她感受到他五根手指的力量透过那件薄薄的黄色连衣裙传来。

"我真的很喜欢你的裙子。" 他低声说。

他的拇指开始微微移动,轻轻滑过她的髋骨。

"真的很甜美。"
"谢谢,但是我……"

她越过他的肩膀,看向通往楼下的门口——但随即,两只手环住了她的腰,她的背已经紧贴在身后的墙上……

"求你了,"她喘息着,唇贴近他的耳边。"我不想,呃……"

Prologue: He Lit Me Like a Match

"Stop it!" The young girl giggled, twisting her shoulder away. "Don't you want to go back down to dance?"

"I like it up here," he shrugged.

She heard the hiss, then saw the flame of a match. Her eyes followed the glow of his cigarette as it moved back and forth in his hands. The roof spread out in a sea of rough concrete, then a sharp drop, then the endless glittering city. Lots of cars moved below, but the air up here was black and still. A tingling feeling came, of lights coming down in a crowded theater...

"Okay, well I think I'll..."

She stepped to the side. But then there was his hand—tight around her hip.

"Hey, don't go," he said casually.

She felt the pressure of five fingers through her flimsy yellow sundress.

"I really do like your dress," he whispered.

His thumb began to move slightly, running over her hipbone.

"It's very sweet."

"Thanks, but I..."

She looked past his shoulder, towards the door leading back downstairs—but then, the sudden feeling of two hands encircling the small of her waist, and her back was already up against the wall behind her...

"Please," she breathed. Her lips were right by his ear. "I don't, um..."

她的项链被卡在了细细的裙带里,迫使她的头以一种尴尬的角度向后仰。她的喉咙里有一种强烈的脉动感。

"没事的。" 他轻声说道。"一切都好。"

她试图调整姿势,猛地拉起肩膀。随之而来的是布料撕裂的声音——

"不,我的裙子,我……"

——她的手本能地飞快护住了胸口,突然暴露在寒冷的夜风中。然而,他敏捷地抓住了她的手腕,用一只手巧妙地将她的双腕固定在腰后。

"别担心," 他笑了笑,"你这样很好看。"

她避开他的眼神,意识到自己那小小的白皙胸部正暴露在外,她觉得自己仿佛成了"展示品"。她的脸烧得发烫,呼吸急促。有人会看到她这样吗?离这里不远的地方,几栋高楼大厦的窗户在明亮的荧光灯下闪着光。

"而且,你没穿胸罩,挺酷的。"

她的眼睛因为过度眨眼而发涩,泪水模糊了视线。她茫然地感觉到他的膝盖挤进了她的双腿之间,慢慢将她抬起,她的小白球鞋的鞋尖几乎悬空。此时,她的裙子变成了一块皱缩在腰间的黄色布料。双臂被扭在身后的姿势让她的胸部不由自主地向前挺出,臀部往下倾斜,紧贴着他的上大腿。她努力想保持平衡,但越是挣扎,越是能感觉到他粗糙的牛仔裤摩擦着她薄薄的棉质内裤。她听见自己发出了一声尖锐的轻呼。她的嘴大概是张开的,因为突然有手指伸进了她的嘴里……

Her necklace had gotten caught in the thin strap of her dress, forcing her head back at an awkward angle. Something pulsed hard in her throat.

"It's okay," he said quietly. "Everything's okay."

She struggled towards a more upright position, pulling her shoulder up sharply. She heard a rip of a fabric—

"No, my dress, I..."

—and her hands flew up to cover her chest, suddenly exposed to the cold night air. But he caught them deftly; with one hand, he pinned both of her wrists neatly behind the small of her back.

"Don't worry," he laughed. "You look good like that."

She looked away from his eyes, painfully aware of her small white breast, she thought, 'on display.' Her face felt hot; her breath came quickly. Could people see her like this? There were bright windows not too far, tall office buildings lit by fluorescent overheads.

"And it's cool you didn't wear a bra."

Her eyes were stinging, blinking too much. Limply, she perceived his thigh pushing up between her knees, prying them open and then lifting her, kind of, so only the very tips of her small white sneakers were touching the ground. Her dress was now just a bit of yellow fabric pooling uselessly around her waist. The position of her arms behind her back was making her chest arch uncomfortably and her hips tilt downwards, forcing her against his upper thigh. It was hard to balance—the more she squirmed to free herself, the more she could feel the raw denim of his jeans, grinding against her roughly through the thin fabric of her cotton underwear. She heard herself make a high noise. Her mouth must have been open, because now there were fingers inside it...

Little Pink Book ~ Olivia Kan-Sperling

"嘘……"

他的手指干燥且有些粗糙,而她的嘴却温暖湿润。她停下了挣扎。

"很好。"

然后,他的手移到她的下颌,轻轻托起她的脸。他把她散落在眼前的头发拨到一边,把长长的发丝塞到了她的耳后。她抬眼看着他。

他的眼睛很深邃。他的手指轻轻拂过她的眉毛,然后是她的眼睑,闭上了她的双眼。她打了个冷颤,顺从地闭上了眼睛。

现在,眼前一片漆黑。她感觉到夜风轻抚着皮肤,手腕被紧紧地握住。她能感觉到另一只手的手指在她的五官上游走——鼻子、嘴唇、颧骨——她知道,他正盯着她看。

"Shhh..."

His fingers were dry and a little chapped; she knew her mouth was wet and warm. She stopped moving.

"That's good."

Then his hand was around her jaw, guiding her face up towards his. He brushed her hair from where it had fallen into her eyes, tucking the long strands behind each ear. She looked up at him.

His eyes were dark. His hand brushed lightly over her brows, then her eyelids, closing her eyes. She shivered. She allowed them to shut.

Now it was black. She was aware of the cool air touching her skin, the hand tight around her wrists. She could feel the fingers of the other running over the contours of her features—nose, lips, cheekbones—and it was like he could see her.

PART 1: ROMANTIC, SENSITIVE, ARTISTIC

~ French Film Proverb ~

"To be chaste is to know every possibility."
—Jean-Luc Godard

第一部分: 浪漫、敏感、艺术气息

~ 法国电影谚语 ~

"贞洁就是了解每一种可能性。"
—让·吕克·戈达尔

第一章: 生活什么时候才能找到我?

"请给我来一杯浪漫薰衣草玫瑰拿铁,不过不要加薰衣草。"那位带着一只小脏狗的女人说道。

"哦,能不能比上次凉一些?上次太烫了,烫伤了我的嘴!"

黄黎美内心深处叹了口气。今天,软滤书法咖啡馆的顾客比平常更加挑剔!也许是湿气,渗透进了每个人的脾气里。

外面的永嘉路上,季风的雨点如银色闪光般扫过温暖的黄色窗户。即使是在下午,天空也呈现出抑郁般的深灰色。

外面的世界就像我心情的写照! 黎美想道。*所有一切都如同复制般相似,真是无比令人厌倦!*

与此同时,黎美努力操控着那台巨大的金属咖啡机。她下眼睑的淡紫色半月痕迹显得憔悴不堪。她推了推圆形的发光眼镜,揉了揉疲惫的双眼,将起泡的白色牛奶缓缓倒入黑色的咖啡中,然后熟练地在泡沫上划出几道线,最终画出了一颗完美的心形。

她将杯子转来转去,观察着自己的作品。没有缺口的心形,算得上是完美吗?她灵巧地为它添加了一支箭的最后点缀。

因为她纤细、灵活而精巧的双手,黄黎美是软滤书法咖啡馆里最出色的拿铁艺术师。她的创作想象力丰富、敏感而富有表现力,深受顾客喜爱。

这天星期一,她面前已经完成了第一百杯浪漫薰衣草玫瑰拿铁。

这不可能就是我来这里的原因吧,她想着。*生活何时才能找到我?*

Chapter 1: When Will Life Ever Find Me?

"One Romance Lavender Rose Surprising Latte, please—*without* the lavender!" said the woman with the small dirty dog.

"Oh, and can you make it cooler than last time? It was so warm it burned my mouth!"

Limei sighed deep down inside. The customers at Soft Filter Calligraphic Coffee Shop were even more demanding than usual today! Maybe it was the humidity, getting under everyone's skin.

On Yongjia Road, monsoon rains swept the cozy yellow windows with silver shivers. Even in the afternoon, the sky was dark gray, depression color.

The outside is like an exact symbol of my mental state! Limei thought. *How dreadfully identical everything is!*

Meanwhile, Limei struggled to operate the huge metal coffee machine. Pale magenta moons groaned under her lower lashes. She pushed up her luminous circular spectacles to rub at her eyes, poured the frothing white milk over the brilliant black coffee, and pirouetted several lines through the foam, executing a perfect heart.

Turning the cup this way and that, she observed her creation. What was a heart without a hole? With dutiful deftness, she ornamented the final flourish of an arrow.

Due to her slender, delicate, and nimble fingers, Huang Limei was the most skilled latte calligrapher at Soft Filter Calligraphic Coffee Shop. She was also the most beloved, being known as well for her particularly imaginative, sensitive, and expressive creations.

On this Monday, she set her one hundredth Romance Lavender Rose Surprising Latte down before her.

至少,班快要结束了...像往常一样,黎美昨晚没怎么睡好,她熬夜和自己的博客"聊天"。这是她在上海唯一的朋友。

~ 六个月前... ~

"哎呀!黎美,你怎么能这样对我?你真是让我心碎!"黄妈妈说道。

"你在电气工程方面那么优秀!"黄爸爸说道,"怎么能想着去当歌手?去出卖自己?"

黎美一把摔上卧室的门,像个星形天使般躺在床上,陷入了她父母永远无法理解的思绪中......

这些闪闪发光的念头自动开始在她的脑海中旋转,像游乐园里的旋转木马一样,变换着形态,但总会回到原点。这就是黎美知道的:

她与众不同.

~ 回到现在 ~

最后一只宠物狗消失在了夏日的夜晚中。黎美脱下了白色围裙,露出了一条蓝色牛仔短裤。

街道两旁,法国梧桐树枝交织,形成了一顶异国情调的绿色屋顶。透过树叶,隐约可以看到一丝丝月光在微笑。街道两旁,法国梧桐树枝交织,形成了一顶异国情调的绿色屋顶。透过树叶,隐约可以看到一丝丝月光在微笑。

This can't be why I'm here, she thought. *When will life ever find me?*

At least it was the end of her shift soon. As usual, Limei hadn't slept too much last night, as she had been up late, talking to her blog. This was her only friend in Shanghai.

~ Six Months Ago... ~

"A-ya! How can you do this to me, Limei? You are breaking my heart!" Mrs. Huang said.

"You are so good at electrical engineering!" said Mr. Huang. "How could you desire to become a singer? Prostituting yourself?"

Slamming her bedroom door behind her, Limei fell on her bed in the shape of an angel star and then, into the kinds of thoughts her parents would never understand...

Automatically, these scintillations began revolving through her mind like the beasts in a carnival carousel—taking different forms, but always coming back around. This is how Limei knew:

She was different.

~ Present Day ~

When the last lapdog scampered off into the summer evening, Limei tore off her white pinafore, revealing blue denim cutoff shorts.

In the air outside, water droplets rubbed together, giving the atmosphere a blurry, romantic filter effect. French parasol trees fashioned themselves into an exotic green roof above the twilit streets. Through their leaves smiled small glowing glimpses of moonshine. The cicadas who lived in these branches, however, were invisible.

三道条纹的运动鞋踩在蒸腾的路面上,黎美时而进入,时而走出一片片轰鸣声。

黎美不禁打了个寒颤。她怕虫子——任何丑陋的东西。

但这种黑暗电力般的强烈声响也激起了她内心深处某种隐藏的情感……

一滴汗珠悄然顺着她的脊背滑落。

为了抵御这种穿透力极强的声响,她戴上了可爱的笨重耳机,开始听音乐。抒情的旋律像一朵柔软、烟雾般的茶花,在她体内缓缓展开,木质吉他的温暖深色调,舒缓着她的心灵。熟悉的旋律让她回想起她热爱的每一件事物。红色罂粟的简单乐趣,放学后吃的多汁桃子,紧紧编成两个蝴蝶结的辫子。

尽管生活在城市里,黎美依然是个土生土长的中国乡村女孩。

这是一首悲伤的歌,就像黎美喜欢听的所有歌曲一样,诉说着痛苦的爱。

但悲伤,是黎美最喜欢的食物。

As her three-striped sneakers pressed on the steaming pavement, Limei was transported in and out of zones of loud buzzing.

Limei shuddered. She was afraid of insects—*anything ugly*.

Though this overwhelming sound of dark electric power also stimulated something deep inside her...

A bead of sweat traced a secret down her spine.

As protection against this penetrating sound, she put on her cute clunky headphones. Lyricism now expanded like a soft, smoky tea flower in Limei, soothing her with the honey-dark color of an acoustic guitar. The familiar flavors of the song reminded her of everything she loved. The simple pleasures of red poppies. Juicy peaches eaten after school. Hair braided tightly into two tight bows.

Though she lived in the city, Limei was still a real Chinese country girl at heart.

This was a sad song, like all the music Limei liked to listen to, telling of a terrible love.

But sadness was Limei's favorite food.

第二章: 笔记本摄像头与可爱的拼贴画

在高中时期,黎美是全班的歌唱、舞蹈、表演偶像。但在上海,她并不是。唯一为她点亮的,是她街道入口处的自动探照灯。

黎美走过刺眼的灯光,走过沉重的大门。那扇门敞开着,上面装饰着一个铁制的心形图案,像一位少女失去了钥匙的日记本。

她礼貌地点了点头,向门口昏昏欲睡的警卫致意。黎美住在法租界的一栋老式住宅楼里。这里,古老弄堂里的简朴家居,依旧点缀着隐秘晾晒的衣物。每个角落都有盆栽等待着欢迎,连摩托车都显得温和可亲。这个世界,像是孩子们的魔法电影,万物都带有友善的面孔。换句话说,这里很孤独,几乎没有真正活生生的人。

黎美蹑手蹑脚地爬上她和室友共用的楼梯。她的室友很少露面。那个小厨房属于她们两人,但实际上却谁也不用。回到自己的房间,黎美会拆开之前买的桃子形状的馒头,像她曾无数次观看的台湾电影中的某个瘾子一样,一片片地撕开蓬松的白色面皮。桃子象征着长生不老,黎美喜欢象征物。她喜欢事物有意义,甚至充满意义。

房间的门轻轻地关上了。因为黑暗,屋里显得空荡荡的。只有天花板上的风扇在嗡嗡作响,像某个不远处的灰尘猫在轻轻地打呼噜。然后黎美打开了灯,屋里并没有猫。

她的房间凌乱不堪: 一个单身女孩在孤独世界中的典型少女闺房。

窗外,雨开始在城市中飘落。

Chapter 2: Laptop Camera and Cute Collage

In high school, Limei had been the singing, dancing, and acting idol of her whole class. In Shanghai, she was not. The only thing that lit up for Limei was the automated floodlight at the entrance to her street.

Limei walked through the glare, then through the heavy gate. It was wide open and decorated with an iron heart, like a young girl's diary that has lost its key.

She nodded politely to the sleepy policeman stationed at the entrance. Limei lived in an old-fashioned housing block in the French Concession. Here, modest homes in historical alleys were still decorated with discreetly dancing laundry lines. Potted plants waited in welcome in every corner. Even the motorcycles seemed nice. This world was like a magical movie for children where things wear the faces of friendly characters. In other words, it was lonely, and there were not many really living people.

Limei crept up the stairs of the place she shared. Her roommate rarely came out. The small kitchen was for both of them, which meant neither of them. In her room, Limei would unwrap a peach-shaped bun and pick out fluffy white pieces like a cripple in a Taiwanese movie she watched so many times. Peaches symbolize immortality. Limei liked things to have meanings.

The bedroom's door clicked softly shut. Because it was dark, the room was empty. Only the ceiling fan whirred above, like a dusty cat purring somewhere close by. Then Limei turned on the light, and there was no cat.

Her room was chaotically kept: the girly room of a single girl who is all alone in the lonely world.

In the square window, rain began to fall on the city.

黎美的心很大，但她的床却太小。床的上方是一幅美丽的拼贴画，撕碎的图片流淌下来，几乎蔓延到枕头上。有王菲可爱的面庞，张曼玉迷茫的脸庞，纳塔莉亚·金斯基金发的轮廓。她曾把杂志撕成碎片，用一种梦幻的方式将它们拼凑在一起。这些图像堆积如愿望池中的硬币，成为她秘密的插图。矛盾的是，这些也都是广为人知的、她最喜欢的电影，如《花样年华》、《中国姑娘》或《银翼杀手》。这些不相干的东西通过形状各异的贴纸拼凑在一起。

显然，这个女孩虽然并非残疾，却充满了创造力和复杂性。

在所有的照片中，黎美最喜欢凝视的是阮玲玉——中国电影史上的著名默片明星。那个年代，明星们不必出声说话，因为字幕会替她们表达。她只需被看到，便能被理解。她是黑白的，像一本书，但在阮玲玉的微笑与悲伤的眼神中，灰色比任何现代色彩更闪耀。

黎美最喜欢的阮玲玉电影是《新女性》，其中她饰演了一位因社会压迫而服用安眠药自杀的解放女性角色。这也是另一位女演员艾霞的真实人生故事。艾霞在21岁时吞食生鸦片自杀。阮玲玉在《新女性》首映不久后，自己也服用安眠药自杀。据说这是因为媒体对她私生活的无情披露，但也可能与她在《新女性》中扮演的角色有关。她当时年仅24岁。据黎美所知，她的葬礼在上海有10万人参加，仪式持续了三天，送葬队伍长达三英里。在此期间，受她启发，有三名女性自杀殉情。

黎美很喜欢这个故事，它非常直接。

Limei's heart was big, but her bed was small. Above it was a
wonderful fresco of ripped images bleeding down the walls and
almost onto the pillow. There was the cute face of Faye Wong and
the cloudy face of Maggie Cheung, the blonde face of Nastassja
Kinski. She had torn magazines asunder and used them in a
dreamy way. These images were heaped like pennies in a wishing
fountain, becoming illustrations of her most personal secrets.
Paradoxically, they were also widely-known, famous films which
were her favorites, such as *In the Mood for Love*, *La Chinoise*, or
Blade Runner. There were many-shaped stickers in between to
hold together these disconnected things.

Clearly, this girl, although not a cripple, was creative and
complicated.

Of all the distressed photographs, Limei most liked to gaze at
Ruan Lingyu, the famous silent star of Chinese cinema. In those
days, a star did not speak out loud. Due to the invention of title
cards, she did not have to. Words might be shown over or after her
image, but they did not belong to her at all. She could simply be
seen, then be understood, and these two things, everyone knew,
were different. Ruan Lingyu was black and white, like a book, but
in her smiles and sad eyes, gray glowed more than any modern
color.

Limei's favorite movie of Ruan Lingyu was *New Women*, in which
an emancipated female character kills herself with sleeping pills
due to society. This was the real life story of another actress,
Ai Xia, who fatally ate raw opium at twenty-one. Ruan Lingyu,
soon after the premiere of *New Women*, herself was suicided with
sleeping pills. This was because of the media tabloids exposing
her most private life, but perhaps also due to the role of the New
Woman she had played. She was twenty-four. Her funeral in
Shanghai was attended by 100,000 people—Limei had read this.
The service lasted three days and the procession, three miles.
Three women killed themselves during the event out of sheer
inspiration.

Limei loved this story. It was very straightforward.

在这面墙上，阮玲玉的照片定格在她身穿校服的样子中。她看起来像一台玩具宝丽来相机般可爱而俏皮。

与此同时，我们的黎美坐在床上，打开了她的笔记本电脑。她是个内敛而神秘的人，但却有一个公开的博客，记录着她的想法——通常是关于她自己、她的生活，黎美的生活。

黎美是独特的，而今晚也是独特的，因为今晚，黎美将发布她的第一段视频。笔记本电脑的摄像头亮起了绿色的灯光，稳定、明亮、耐心且真诚。她拿出了吉他，开始唱歌。当她唱完时，停止了录制。

随后，她闭上双眼，甜甜地微笑，然后进入梦乡。

On this girl's wall, Ruan Lingyu was captured as a young star in a school uniform. She looks as playful and easy to use as a toy polaroid camera.

Meanwhile, our Limei sat down on the bed and lit up her laptop. She was an intense and secretive person, so Limei had a public blog of thoughts. The thoughts were usually about herself, her life, the life of Limei.

Limei was unique and tonight was also unique, because Limei was going to post her very first video upload. The green light of her laptop camera held steady and bright. She took out her guitar and began to sing. When she was done, she stopped the recording.

Then she closed her eyes, smiled sweetly, and slept.

第三章: 桃色夜晚

你好啊,那个我永远无法成为的女孩
阳光洒在她的头发上,快乐而自由
她走路像水,谈笑间如乐音
从不考虑清晨的到来

花园里高高的桃子
从未被吃掉,它们从未凋零
那它们究竟有何滋味
所有的美丽,难道全是浪费?

一个男孩从大屏幕上俯瞰
他说嗨,他给我买了冰淇淋
但我醒来,只是一场白日梦

生活在我的脑海中
我从不怀疑
安全而稳妥,但我
希望你能把我带出来……

转过身来,请注意我
对我这样的女孩来说,别无他法
没有人能用他的目光让我自由
孤单的夜晚,唯有一物映入眼帘……

一颗雪白的桃子,与你分享!
还有桃花肌肤的夜晚,献给你!
一颗雪白的桃子,与你分享!
玫瑰色的光辉,还有黎明的露珠!

他们说我应该耐心等待
照顾花园,锁好大门
但我想要迎接我的命运
请快点,在为时已晚之前!

一颗雪白的桃子,与你分享……
还有桃花肌肤的夜晚,献给你……
你,你,你,你……

Chapter 3: Peach Skin Nights

Hello there, girl I'll never be
Sun in her hair, happy and free
Walks like water, talks like laughter
Never thinks about the morning after

Peaches in the garden way up high
Never eaten, they never die
So do they even have a taste
All their beauty, all a waste?

A boy looked down from the big screen
He said hi, he bought me ice cream
But I woke up, just a daydream

Living in my mind
I never have to doubt
Safe and sound but I
Wish you'd tear me out...

Turn around, please just notice me
There's nothing else for a girl like me to be
And no one else whose look will set me free
Alone at night, only one thing I see...

A peach, snow-white, to share with you!
And peach skin nights to give to you!
A peach, snow-white to share with you!
Rosy light, and dawn's first dew!

They say it's nice for me to wait
Mind the garden, lock the gate
But I want to meet my fate
Hurry, please, before it's too late!

A peach, snow-white, to share with you...
And peach skin nights to give to you...
You, you, you, you...

第四章：甜梦造型

在她的粉色毯子下，黎美穿着一条浅黄色的内裤，外面搭配黑色的绒面睡裤。束带紧贴在她纤细的臀部。黎美的睡眠面罩紧紧包裹着她的双眼。她的薄袜子刚好到达脚踝骨下方，随着她的睡姿轻柔地摩擦着彼此…

Chapter 4: Sweet Dreams Outfit

Under her pink blanket, Limei was wearing a pair of light yellow underwear and, over them, black velour sleep shorts. The drawstring band fit snugly around her slim hips. Limei wore a sleeping mask wrapped tightly around her eyes. Her thin socks ending just below her ankle bone, moved against each other softly as she slept...

第五章: 秘密梦境造型

在夜晚明亮的灯光下,黎美穿着一袭黑色丝绸旗袍,绣有红色和金色的龙。立领紧束着她的呼吸,让她难以歌唱。或者她穿着一件覆盆子色的兔毛毛衣,湿润的气息在她柔嫩的奶白肌肤上轻轻流淌。又或者她穿着一条银色亮片裙,粗犷无比,下面什么也没有,搭配着一头短短的金色波波头。可是,她常常会剪成一款短粉色波波头。她也常常穿着蓝色天鹅绒的衣服。或者是一条浅婴儿蓝色的迷你裙,搭配婴儿蓝色的紧身裤和一件紧身白色开衫。也许她还会在这一切上面穿着一件透明的塑料雨衣。总是弥漫着浓厚的蓝色烟雾,窗帘和破碎的镜子。而伴随其中的还有爵士乐的旋律。

Chapter 5: Secret Dreams Outfit

Under the night's bright lights, Limei was wearing a black satin qipao embroidered with red and gold dragons. The mandarin collar constricted her breath, making it difficult to sing. Or she was wearing a raspberry-color rabbit fur sweater, breathing humidly on her soft, milk skin. Or she was wearing a silver sequined dress, very rough, and nothing underneath, and a short blond bob. But often, she was wearing a short pink bob. Often she was wearing blue velvet. Or she was wearing a light-baby-blue minidress, baby-blue tights, and a tight, white wrap sweater. Maybe she was wearing a see-through plastic raincoat over all of this. Always there was lots of blue cigarette smoke, curtains, and a broken mirror. And there was...jazz music, too...

第六章: 黎美的秘密梦境生活我?

"十分钟后上场,黎黎!"老板艾迪透过一串廉价的塑料珠帘大喊。珠帘在门口泛着紫色的光芒,轻轻地撩拨着门槛,像假睫毛一样调皮又诱惑。

站在更衣室里,黎美给眼睛涂上了眼影。

今晚在中国玫瑰顶级私人俱乐部,其他女孩们在背景中忙碌着。她们脱下战斗靴,换上高跟鞋和迷你衣服,通常是黑色的,紧紧包裹着颜色鲜艳的胸罩和内裤。那些女孩多是俄罗斯、泰国或越南籍的。为她们准备的金属储物柜又小又硬,但没有锁。柜子里通常藏着一瓶用秘密卫衣包裹的伏特加。黎美一般从来不喝这瓶酒。这是因为黎美是特别的,绝对不会那样做!

当黎美走出更衣室时,她避免与阴暗走廊中的人眼神接触。尽管光线昏暗,墙壁上却明显贴满了英女王、金刚和美元的贴纸,红色和黑色的设计像是美国街头艺术家的作品,繁杂的图案掩盖不住粉色灯光背后暴露出的通往私人房间的秘密轮廓,那里是"重要人士"的专属区域,正如任何看过她博客的读者所知,黎美从未进入过。

漫长的黑暗走廊尽头挂着一帘厚重的黑幕。黎美轻轻触碰那粗糙的黑天鹅绒,感受到历史的厚重气息。她偷偷探头看了过去。

中国玫瑰的主舞池是一片硬木地板,正中央悬挂着一盏华丽的吊灯。舞池延伸至无尽的阴影中,没有墙壁或角落。两人桌椅错落有致,小舞台上,Billy正弹奏着黑色钢琴。舞台的灯光刺眼,黎美无法看清观众的面孔,甚至无法确认他们是否真的在场。但她当然可以想象他们的模样。

Chapter 6: Limei's Secret Dream Life

"Ten minutes and you're on, Lily!" Eddy, the boss, yelled through the trashy fringe of plastic beads. Purpling the doorway, they tickled its threshold ever so gently, like fake and flirtatious eyelashes.

Standing still in a changing room, Limei applied a shadow to her eyes.

As usual, tonight at China Rose Paramount Private Club, other girls were in the background. They were yanking off combat boots and strapping into heels and mini clothes, usually black, that bandaged over bras and panties, usually colorful. The girls were usually Russian, Thai, or Vietnamese. There were small, hard metal lockers for the girls, but there were no locks. There was usually a bottle of vodka wrapped in a secret sweatshirt. Usually, Limei never, ever drank from it. This is because Limei was special and would never do that!

As Limei left the room of girls, she averted her eyes from those of the horrible hallway, which, though dim, was unmistakably wall-papered with sticker decals of the Queen of England, King Kong, and dollar bills, done in the red and black style of an American street artist and failing to disguise through their busy pattern the pink light betraying the secret outlines of the doors leading into private rooms reserved for "Very Important Persons" that Limei, as any reader of her blog would know, had never, ever entered.

The long, dark hallway ended in a long, dark curtain. Limei touched her cheek to the rough black velvet, which was hung very heavy. She peered around it.

The main dance floor of China Rose was a hardwood expanse under a big chandelier. Receding forever, it ended in dark shadows, instead of walls or corners. There were chairs and tables for two, and a small stage with a black piano played by Billy. There was a glare from the stage lighting, so Limei could never see the faces of the audience, neither what they looked like, nor whether they were there at all. But, of course, she could imagine them.

再过一会儿，艾迪就会调暗大吊灯，然后打开聚光灯，黎美便会在曲线优美的钢琴旁缓缓走出。

她将与光中的飞蛾相聚。

接着，黎美会抬起头，慢慢地，轻轻地将涂着亮漆的唇瓣贴上冰冷的金属麦克风。

In a moment, Eddy would dim the big chandelier. Then he would hit the stage spotlight, causing Limei to appear by slinking her way around the curvy piano.

She would join the moths under the light.

Then, Limei would lift her head. So slowly, she would part her lacquered lips against the cold metal microphone.

第七章: 再一次, 再一次, 再一次
（我想感受你的车灯照在我的脸上）

白云城, 夜色如墨
我喝酒以便不去思考
你的车子在每个拐角轻盈滑过……
平滑无声, 如同黑豹……
什么时候会打动我？
（告诉我, 宝贝, 什么时候会打动我）
请, 亲爱的, 别太快
我想感受你的车灯照在我的脸上
就像你曾经指尖勾勒的方式
我的下巴, 我的唇, 它们的形状
像录像带一样重播
当一切终于解开
在你的聚光灯下我被迷住
我知道那时我会知道恐惧
希望那时我会知道恐惧
再一次, 再一次, 再一次——

Chapter 7: Again, Again, Again
(I Want to Feel Your Headlights on My Face...)

White cloud city, night as ink
I drink so I don't have to think
How your car glides round every cornerrrr...
Smooth and silent like a pantherrrr...
When will it hit me?
(Tell me, baby, when will it hit me)
Please, honey, not too quickly
I want to feel your headlights on my face
The way your fingers used to trace
My jaw, my lips, their shape
Replayed like a video, video tape
And when it finally comes unwound
And in your spotlights I'm spellbound
I know I'll know fear then
Hopefully, I'll know fear then
Again, again, again—

PART 2: HEAVY-HANDED

~ Second Confucian Proverb ~

"Words are the voice of the heart."
—Confucius

第二部分: 用力过猛

~ 第二句孔子箴言 ~

"言语是心灵的声音。"
—孔子

第八章: 一件充满图案的T恤

24小时不间断,黎美在咖啡的舞蹈中翩翩起舞。她的手如蝴蝶般灵动,优雅地在浓缩咖啡机上飞舞,宛如一位电子组装工;她的刷子在浓郁的咖啡中旋转,仿佛一位老道的艺术家。就这样,她在咖啡杯的卡布奇诺中,创作出一首又一首的诗。

"这是我送给你的诗,"她意味深长地说道。

"希望你喜欢这首惊喜的诗,"她惊喜地说。

"午后的诗就像满月下的爱情,"她感伤地说道。

软过滤书法咖啡馆"的新奇之处不仅在于将传统书法应用于拿铁艺术——真正的亮点在于每一杯创作都是百分之百独特的。就像一首诗。员工们穿着印有"哦,你能给我加个惊喜吗?"的T恤。

一位女士点了一杯带有贵宾犬图案的咖啡。一位商人得到了"好运"咖啡。

顾客们信任并期待黎美为他们制作的不仅是一杯提神的咖啡,而是一杯从未见过的拿铁,他们想象着每一杯都能表达这位美丽女咖啡师敏感的灵魂……

但黎美知道,只有特别的人才能配得上特别的咖啡。

*一个英俊的陌生人带我离开这里……*她想着,手中轻巧地搅拌着三片抹茶粉,营造出一个完美野餐的奶白场景。 *那才是一个惊喜!*

就在这时,书法咖啡馆的大门猛地打开,发出一声巨响。

46 小粉书

Chapter 8: A Very Graphic T-Shirt

24/7, Limei danced her choreography of coffee. Her hands butterflied over the espresso machine with the wit and grace of an electronics assembler; her brush swirled through the dark java with the wisdom of an old master. Like this, she created poem after poem within the pale lunar plane of the coffee cup's cappuccino.

"Here, a poem from me to you," she said insightfully.

"I hope you enjoy this surprising poem," she said amazingly.

"A poem in the afternoon is like love by full moon," she said wistfully.

The novelty trick of Soft Filter Calligraphic Coffee Shop was not only the application of traditional calligraphy to latte art—the true bonus was that each creation was one hundred percent unique, just like a poem. The employees wore t-shirts that said, "Oh, and Can You Put a Surprise On That?"

A lady got a coffee with a poodle in it. A businessman got a coffee of "Good Fortune."

The customers trusted and desired for Limei to make them not only a coffee to energize their senses, but a never-before-seen latte, each one, they imagined, expressive of this beautiful barista's sensitive soul...

But Limei knew that only a very special person could ever deserve a special coffee.

A handsome stranger to take me away from here...she thought, whisking three blades of matcha green into a milky scene of a perfect picnic. *Now that would be a surprise!*

Just then, the door to the Calligraphic banged open with a burst.

"啊!" 黎美惊呼,撒了一地的姜黄蜂蜜糖浆,沾满了她的围裙。

谁这么粗鲁地推开门? 她嘟囔着,低头去捡起掉落的东西。

当她的头从柜台后抬起时,她的目光被一双敏感、讽刺、优雅、聪明而又强大的眼睛锁住,仿佛被囚禁。

那是一个男孩。他独自站在风吹动的入口处,嘴角挂着一抹微笑。他的T恤上印着一张女人的照片,钱币从她的嘴里滑出,塞进她蕾丝内衣里。照片上方用强烈的白色字母斜斜地写着:"*卧虎藏龙,泪猫。*"他英俊得令人心动。夏雨滴落在地板上,而他对此造成的混乱毫不在意。

"Ahhhh!" Limei gasped, spilling turmeric-honey syrup all down the front of her pinafore.

Who would use a door so rudely? She grumbled, ducking down to pick up what she had dropped.

When her head rose up above the counter, her gaze was arrested and imprisoned by a pair of sensitive, sarcastic, elegant, intelligent, and powerful eyes.

They belonged to a boy. Alone, he stood at the windy entrance with a smirk. His t-shirt displayed a photograph of a woman with dollar bills sliding out of her mouth and stuffed into her lacy lingerie. Over her image, strong white letters slanting against rectangular red proposed: *Crouching Tiger, Crying Kitten*. Summer rain dripped to the floor. He was handsome. And he did not look sorry for the mess he had forced her to make.

第九章：粗鲁的男孩

"对不起,"黎美对那个点了"可爱荔枝水煮蛋拿铁"的人说道。"我把东西洒了。"

所以,黎美不得不重新开始。繁琐的荔枝水煮蛋拿铁包含了椰子和姜黄风味的奶泡,还有一圈荔枝"辣酱"。这些成分当然形成了一个蛋的形状,就像名字所说的那样。但为什么咖啡上面要放一个蛋呢?这是黎美最讨厌的订单,任何读过她博客的人都知道。

她能感觉到排队的无礼男孩用目光盯着她,还在笑。她感觉到粘稠的糖浆顺着她的T恤滴下来。她想找个借口换衣服,但黎美知道绝不能让顾客久等。

"请问,我可以为您做什么,先生?"

"嗯……"年轻男孩说,手指轻轻捻着下巴,似乎想要花点时间决定。

"我想……要一个'可爱荔枝水煮蛋拿铁'!"他说,带着得意的口气。"……麻烦了。"

"哦,你能给我加个惊喜吗?" 他眨了眨眼. "随便你觉得适合我的。"

黎美在心中怒火中烧,手中的搅拌动作也变得激烈。这个人的脸上有种让她感到疯狂的东西。她将姜黄、牛奶、荔枝糖浆和浓缩咖啡混在一起……

"这是你的诗,"她带着一丝态度说道。"希望你喜欢。"

无礼的男孩深深地盯着杯子。

Chapter 9: Rude Boy

"I'm sorry," Limei said to the person who had chosen to order a Lovely Litchi Poached Egg Latte. "I've spilled."

So Limei had to begin all over again. The laborious Lovely Litchi Poached Egg Latte included both coconut- and turmeric-flavored milk foam, plus a swirl of litchi "hot sauce." These ingredients, of course, made a picture of an egg, just like the name said. But why? It was stupid, and it was Limei's most hated order, as any reader of her blog would know.

She could feel the rude boy, next in line, leave his eyes on her and laugh. She felt sticky syrup drip down inside her t-shirt. She wanted to excuse herself in order to change, but Limei knew to never keep a customer waiting.

"What may I make for you, sir?"

"Hm...." The young man said, tapping his finger on his chin in order to take a long time to decide.

"I think... I'll have... one of those Lovely Litchi Poached Egg Lattes!" he said triumphantly. "...Please."

"Oh, and can you put a Surprise on that?" he added with a wink. "Whatever you think suits me perfectly."

Limei seethed around, swirling. There was something in this person's face that made her feel crazy. She mixed together turmeric and milk, litchi syrup and espresso....

"Here's your poem," she said with a flash of attitude. "I hope you like it."

The rude boy looked deep into the cup.

He smiled even more at the sight of Limei's bratty creation.

Instead of painting something lovely like hearts or flowers around

当看到黎美调皮的创作时,他的笑容更加灿烂。黎美并没有在这个早餐菜肴的边缘绘制出美丽的心形或花朵,而是把她的刷子戳进了奶泡里,给他呈现了一个做得很糟糕的炒蛋。

"美味,"陌生人说道。"我敢打赌你早上给男朋友做早餐时也很在行。"

她脸上火热的潮红和咖啡因的氛围让她感到不堪重负。看着他挑衅的眉毛,黎美担心他能看透她的单纯......

"你知道他们怎么说的,"他神秘地对她眨了眨眼。"为了做个煎蛋,你得打破几个蛋。"

"哦,还有,你身上沾了......黄色的液体,"他说。"你可能想清理一下,这看起来像是......"

他笑了,然后又一次粗鲁地关上了门。

如同白皙的肌肤,黎美完全不知道他在说什么。她愤怒地看着他离开。她讨厌那些未言明的含义。这样太无礼和懒惰,用半空的意义给人传递信息!

就在这时,她看到柜台上放着一张500元人民币的钞票。她立刻明白这个陌生人是把它留在那里的。作为上海顶级咖啡馆的咖啡师,黎美经常收到那些不知道小费在中国被视为不合适的外国人的小费。但这个男孩显然知道他在做什么。

"他以为我是谁......妓女吗! ?!?"

人们困惑地抬头看向她。

黎美用手捂住了嘴。她太困惑了,以至于没意识到自己已经在出声思考。

52 小粉书

the edges of this morning meal, Limei had stabbed her brush in
the foam, presenting him with a badly-done scrambled egg.

"Yum," said the stranger. "I'll bet you're good at making breakfast for your boyfriend in the morning."

A flush buzzing over her skin added to the unbearably caffeinated
atmosphere. By the way his eyebrows taunted her, Limei feared he
could tell how innocent she really was.

"You know what they say," he winked at her mysteriously. "In
order to make an omelette, you have to break a few eggs."

With a flick of his fine wrist, he tossed a 500RMB note on the
counter. As a barista at a top-tier Shanghai establishment, Limei
often got tips from foreigners who did not know how tipping was
considered inappropriate. Limei, after all, was not a stripclub
dancer. But this boy knew exactly what he was doing!

"Oh, and by the way, you have this...yellow liquid all over you," he
said. "You might want to clean that up, it looks like...."

He laughed. Then he left, slamming the door once more
obnoxiously.

Lily-white Limei had no idea what he was talking about.
Furiously, she watched him go. She hated when meanings were
implied only, and not obvious. It was confusing, perverse, and
immoral. It was rude.

Little Pink Book ~ Olivia Kan-Sperling   53

第十章：淋浴场景

当黎美那天晚上回到自己的房间时，她撕下沾满污垢的衣物，纵身一跃倒在床上。她仰望着贴在天花板上的那些图像。

真是奇怪的一天……

在淋浴时，黎美确保使用大量的肥皂。她从瓶子里挤出泡沫，放在左手中。她杏仁形的指甲在浴室的灯光下散发着健康的光泽。珠光的沐浴露在她轻轻捧起的手心中汇聚成一滩新鲜的粉红牛奶。黎美兴奋地微笑，露出洁白闪亮的牙齿。当她将肥皂抹在光滑如缎的**肌肤**上时，泡沫开始在她的身体上迅速增多，短暂地闪烁出彩虹般的色彩，随后在喷头喷出的热水下融化……浴室里弥漫着蒸汽。

与此同时，清澈的黎美开始哼起一首新歌，因为她喜欢在淋浴时唱歌。

在冲洗完她娇小的身体后，她走出浴室，感觉**干净**清新，宛如新生。她将润肤露涂抹在修长的腿上，然后在一股香甜的糖饼、婴儿爽身粉和茉莉花香气中回到自己的房间。

就在这时，她注意到自己最脏的脏衣物中有一张东西藏着。

"嗯？"

她拿起那张从里边露出的纸质矩形。

"这怎么会在这里？"

那是一张名片，上面印着：

~ *玫瑰百合娱乐。艺人经纪人。* ~

Chapter 10: Shower Scene

When Limei returned to her room that evening, she tore off her soiled clothing and indulged herself by fainting onto her bed. She stared up at the images she'd pasted into the sky.

What a weird day...

In the shower, Limei made sure to use a lot of soap. She squirted the solution from the bottle into her left hand. Her almond-shaped nails glowed healthily in the bathroom light. The pearlescent body wash pooled like a puddle of pink milk in her gently cupped hand. Limei smiled enthusiastically, showing white, flashing teeth. When she smoothed the soap over her slippery, silky, satin skin, loads and loads of bubbles began multiplying and rainbowing over her body, before melting away under the hot water coming out of the shower head.... Steam filled the bathroom.

Meanwhile, limpid Limei began to hum a new song, because she liked to sing in the shower.

After rinsing her petite body, she stepped out feeling very perfectly clean and fresh as new. She dumped lotion over her long legs, then reappeared in her room under a fragrant cloud of sugar cookies, baby powder, and jasmine.

It was then that she noticed something nestled in her most dirty laundry.

"Huh?"

She picked up the paper rectangle poking out.

"How did this get here?"

It was a business card and on it was printed:

~ Rose Lily Entertainment. Talent Agent. ~

上面还有一个号码,以及一行字,潦草而粗犷的笔迹……

我们认为你有很多才华。我们希望能谈谈你在娱乐行业的未来。请拨打电话以安排会议。.

"什么!?!"

她猜想一定是有人在咖啡馆里把这个递给她……可是,谁呢?

她沉思着用柔软的毛巾擦干完美无瑕的身体。

在床头上,许多女孩的目光回望着她。

There was a number, and some more words underneath, written in a messy, masculine hand...

We think you've got a lot of talent.
We'd love to talk about your future in the entertainment industry.
Please call to set up a meeting.

"What!?!"

Someone must have slipped this to her at the café, she guessed... but who?

She finished drying her flawless body thoughtfully with a soft, fluffy towel.

Above the bed, many girls looked back at her.

第十一章：一个出乎意料的问题

当黎美拨打名片上的号码时，一位专业的女士接电话，回答道："玫瑰百合娱乐前台，您好？"她只确认了一个初级星探名叫蒴诗雷注意到了黎美，并希望与她讨论合同。黎美告诉她，由于在咖啡馆工作，她只能在周末见面。秘书表示需要与蒴先生咨询，然后在仅仅二十分钟后再次来电，给了黎美一个会面的时间和地点：周六下午三点，在安福路的一家咖啡店。

接下来的一周仿佛在私人飞机上一晃而过，因此在周六，黎美准时到达那里。蒴诗雷似乎还没到。

黎美四处张望。在街上，其他同龄女孩三三两两地走来走去。许多女孩怀着羡慕的目光凝视着一家优雅时尚的花店的橱窗。黎美也走了过去。她轻轻地用指尖触碰着花瓣，幻想着哪种人将来会给她买这样一束花……

她陶醉于空中的美好梦想中，以至于当她感到一阵温暖的气息在脖子后面吹拂时，她花了太久才从云端坠落，回到现实中反应过来。

她转身，惊叫出声。

"什么！又是你！"

是那个在工作时羞辱过她的无礼男孩！

蒴诗雷穿着休闲，深色牛仔裤和白色Polo衫，嘴角挂着得意的微笑。

"希望有人给你拍照吗？"

脸红的黎美无视了那句话。时尚的安福路是女孩们和朋友们一起拍可爱照片的地方。因此，这里也成了那些不请自来的色老头拍照的臭名昭著的地方……！！

Chapter 11: A Surprising Question

When Limei called the number on the card, a professional lady, answering the phone as "Rose Lily Entertainment front office, hello?" had confirmed only that a junior scout named Kuai Shilei had noticed Limei and would like to discuss a contract with her. Limei told her that she could only meet on weekends, due to her job in a café. The secretary said she had to consult with Mr. Kuai, then called back only twenty minutes later to give Limei a time and a place to meet: a coffeeshop on Anfu Road, 3 p.m. that Saturday.

The rest of the week flew by on a private jetplane, so on Saturday, Limei got there exactly on time. Kuai Shilei seemed to be late.

Limei looked around. In the street, other girls her age blew this way and that. Many of them gazed wistfully into the window of an elegant, cutting-edge florist. Limei approached, too. She permitted her fingers to graze the petals respectfully, picturing the kind of person who might one day buy her such a bouquet...

So lost in sky-high dreams was she that when she felt a warm breath on the back of her neck, it took her too long to fall from her clouds back into the situation to which she had to react in real life.

She turned around, then gasped.

"What! You again!"

It was the rude boy who had **humiliated** her at work!

Kuai Shilei was dressed for casual conversation, in dark jeans, a white polo, and a satisfied smirk.

"Hoping someone will take a photo of you?"

Blushing, Limei ignored the comment. The trendy Anfu Road was where girls went with friends to take cute pictures to post online. For this reason, it had also become a notorious spot for perverted old men to take photos without permission...!!

蒴诗雷的硬朗笑声化作温柔的微笑,接着又变成可爱的皱眉。尽管他的五官棱角分明—高高的颧骨、直挺的鼻子、浓密的眉毛—但他脸上的情绪变化太快,让她根本跟不上。对于黎美来说,人们的情感常常以一种她只能看见而无法解读的语言展现出来。

此时,这个男孩正在咬着下唇,仿佛面临着一个棘手的问题。

"让我想想……我应该给你买一些花吗?"

黎美更加脸红了! 蒴诗雷难道能读懂她的心思? 他似乎精确地回应着她内心深处的细腻情感,像最危险的武术大师一样……

她该怎么回答呢? 甚至承认这个问题都会是错误的答案! 黎美感觉自己被逼到了对话的新角落,甚至没意识到身后还有一堵墙。

幸好,蒴诗雷在他们面前打开了真正的门。黎美跟着他走了进去。

他选择的咖啡馆既新又酷。

"我选这个地方是因为我觉得你会在这样的地方更放松,"蒴诗雷说着,一边为她拉开椅子。"你喜欢咖啡馆,对吧?"

实际上,黎美并不觉得放松。这个地方冷得刺骨,墙壁涂成银色,椅子硬得让人难以坐下。蒴诗雷端着两杯黑咖啡回来,他的脸色又变了。现在,他像个白领专业人士。

"如你所知,我是一名星探。我的工作是寻找特别的年轻人,把他们培养成明星。当我在咖啡馆遇到你时……有什么东西告诉我……你会成为一个不可思议的演员!"

黎美惊呼出声。她回头看去,确保蒴诗雷的话确实是对她说的! 但他们是咖啡馆里唯一的顾客。

Kuai's hard laugh melted into a soft smile, then curled into a cute frown. Though his features were cut sharp and clear—high flat cheekbones, straight nose, dark brow—the emotions they depicted were changing too quickly for her to follow. For Limei, people were often written in a language she could only see, not read.

Now, the guy was biting his lip, as though faced with a tricky problem.

"Let me see... Shall I buy you some flowers?"

Limei **blushed** even harder! Could Kuai Shilei read her mind? He seemed to react with precision to the private movements of her heart and soul, like the most dangerous of martial artists...

What could she say? Even acknowledging the question would be the wrong answer! Limei felt like she was getting **backed** into new corners of the conversation when she hadn't even known there was a wall behind her.

Thankfully, Kuai opened the real door right in front of them. Limei followed him inside.

The café he had chosen was new and cool.

"I picked this spot because I thought you'd feel more comfortable in a place like this," Kuai said, pulling out a chair for her. "You love coffee shops, right?"

In fact, Limei was not comfortable. This location was freezing, the walls painted silver, and the chairs rock-hard. Returning with two black coffees, Kuai's face had switched up again. Now, he was a **white-collar professional**.

"As you know, I'm a talent scout. My job is to find special young people and turn them into stars. When I met you at the café... Something told me... you would make an incredible actress!"

Limei gasped. She looked behind her to make certain Kuai Shilei's remarks were indeed meant for her! But they were the only ones in the café.

咖啡热得烫人。她小心翼翼地抿了一口,以确保这不是梦!嘴巴被烫得火辣辣的—这可不是梦!

蒯诗雷从五英尺外将纸杯扔进垃圾桶,杯子划出一道优美的弧线,然后顺利落入塑料内衬中。他用一次性纸巾消毒了双手。

"如果你感兴趣,我们明天就签合同。"

然后他站起身,黎美仰头看着他。

"你不常外出,对吧?"他微笑着问,"今天是周六,来一起玩吧。"

The coffee was hot. She took a sip to make sure it hurt. Her mouth burned—it was no dream!

Kuai Shilei tossed his paper cup into the trash from five feet away. It arced, then swooshed into the plastic lining. He sanitized his hands with a disposable towelette.

"If you're interested, we'll sign the paperwork tomorrow."

Then he stood. Limei looked up at him.

"You don't go out much, do you?" he smiled kindly. "It's a Saturday. Come have some fun."

第十二章: 一场告白

砰。砰。砰。砰。

黎美再也不知道自己身处何方。低音替代了她的心跳! 夜晚在房间里旋转; 她身在其中。一切都在醉酒, 连黎美自己……

蒯诗雷的一群朋友已经消失。她周围发生着熟悉的事情, 像是美国音乐视频中的场景。沉重的吊灯在她头顶散发光芒。假雾隐藏了舞池的边缘, 甚至渗入她的裙子, 带来一阵清凉的触感, 掠过她的肌肤。

一切都在移动……但似乎什么也没有发生。

黎美含着吸管, 微微噘起嘴。

蒯诗雷到底在哪里? 他毕竟把她带到这里。难道他不应该是个绅士, 照顾她这个无助又孤单的女孩吗?

黎美意识到心中的愤怒正悄然滋生, 并决定把它留着。喝完另一杯酒后, 她开始在雾中穿行。

典型。他不过是个无礼的男孩罢了!

她找到一扇门, 走了进去。现在她身处一个新空间: 更黑, 更冷, 更安静。

黎美咯咯笑着, 嗝了一声, 摇摇晃晃, 失去了方向感。谢天谢地, 男声很快传入她敏感的耳朵, 仍在音乐的余韵中震动。

"哇, 黎美——小心别摔倒。"

蒯诗雷坐在那里……就在那里, 靠近一张低矮的桌子。

原来他一直是一个人……

Chapter 12: The Confession

Boom. Boom. Boom. Boom.

Limei no longer knew what she was inside. The bass had replaced her heartbeat! The night spun around the room; she was inside it. Everything was drunk, even Limei herself...

The group of Kuai's friends had disappeared. Things were happening around her, familiar to Limei from American music videos. A heavy chandelier radiated overhead. Fake fog hid the edges of the dance floor. It even seeped under her dress, stretching a cool sensation over her skin.

Everything was moving...but nothing was happening.

Limei pursed her lips around her straw.

Where was Kuai Shilei, anyway? He had brought her here, after all. Shouldn't he be a gentleman and take care of her, since she was helpless and all alone?

Limei recognized the plausible idea of indignation occurring to her and decided to keep it. Finishing another drink, she started moving through the fog.

Typical. He's just a rude boy after all!

She found a doorway and went through it. Now she was in a new space: darker, cooler, quieter.

Limei giggled and hiccuped. She swayed back, then forth. Thankfully, a male voice soon found her sensitive ear, still vibrating from the music.

"Woah there Limei—don't fall."

Kuai Shilei sat...*there*. There, over there, at a low table.

So he was alone all this time, too...

当黎美站在他面前时,她感到派对的雾气在她周围蒸发。来到这里,她想要离开。但她的话已经开始流露,像路一样铺展开来。

"你以为……你可以……就这样忽视我吗?"

当然,娇小的黎美并不知道如何驾驭这种对话。

"我没想到你这么喜欢我,"他说。

蒴诗雷隐藏在阴影中。但黎美则被派对后面的闪烁灯光照亮。灯光在她身上闪烁,慢动作般地在她面前穿过,冻结了她的表情,像漫画条幅一样——每个表情都拉长,越靠越近……

我根本不认识你,蒴诗雷! 我只是觉得你在晚上邀请我出来,然后不跟我说话,实在不专业!"

从黑暗中,蒴诗雷带着宽容、歉意、讽刺和自嘲的笑声响起。

"你说得对,黎美,我很抱歉。我不是一个好的主人。我该有什么礼貌呢? 来,坐下。再来一杯**桃乌龙马提尼**。"

她看到有一张天鹅绒**沙发**环绕着墙壁。现在,她坐在上面,感觉柔软舒适。

"哦,我真的很喜欢……嗝……桃子……主要是……那个形状……你知道……我每晚吃一个桃子包? 那是我晚餐的食物……"

"哈哈,真好。其实,黎美,我很高兴你来找我。我有一个忏悔……"

蒴诗雷的**低语**如同沙发一样: 粉色而深沉。

As Limei stood before him, she felt the party fog evaporate around her. Having come, she wanted to go. But her words were already happening, unrolling before her like the road.

"You think....you can...just ignore me?"

Of course, little Limei did not know how to drive.

"I didn't think you liked me that much," he said.

Kuai Shilei was in shadow. But Limei was illuminated over and over by the strobing lights of the party background. In slow motion they flashed across her, freezing her face into a comic strip sequence—each expression longer, each one bigger, as Limei got closer—and closer...

"I don't even know you, Kuai Shilei! I just don't think it's very professional for you to invite me out at night and then not even talk to me!"

From the darkness, Kuai laughed graciously, apologetically, sarcastically, and self-deprecatingly.

"You're right, Limei, I'm sorry. I haven't been a very good host. Where are my manners? Come sit down. Have another **Peach Oolong Martini**."

She saw there was a velvet **sofa** wrapped subtly around the walls. Then she was on it, nice and soft.

"Oh, I really like...hic...peaches...mainly...the shape...you know... every night I eat a peach bun? Because I..."

"Haha, cool. Actually, Limei, I'm glad you came to find me. I have a confession to make..."

Kuai's **whispers** sounded like the sofa: pink and deep.

"我绝对不会自己自愿来像'软滤'这样的咖啡店。我不需要一个荔枝拿铁。多么无趣啊。不,我是为了找你而来的……这真是令人尴尬,但我必须承认,我通过你在博客上发布的视频找到了你——就是你在卧室里唱那首歌的视频。我知道我一定得见见你……"

尽管这个英俊的艺人忏悔并不符合他之前的行为,实际上这些行为暗示着完全相反的真相,但对黎美来说,他所说的一切都合乎逻辑,并不令人惊讶,反而愉快地证实了内心与外界两种现实的完美一致,当两者不对齐时,黎美的生活显得特别难以忍受。

"也许你能看出来……我有一种近乎无懈可击的个性。通常,女人们对我很感兴趣。不幸的是,她们却让我感到冷漠。但我必须承认,这首歌激起了我内心深处的某种情感。如此脆弱——纯净——亲密!我感觉像是在遇见一个完全陌生的人,却又仿佛深深地认识他……"

即使黎美一直知道他会这么说,她的心跳还是跟着节拍跳动,正好跟上。

蒴诗雷继续说道:"你一定很有勇气以那种方式展示自己,知道任何人都可以看到你……"

这时,黎美脸红了。在他的目光下,她感到无所适从。音乐如重压般压在她的胸口。她低下头,腼腆地转动着小小的鸡尾酒伞。她感到自己处在一个无论如何都将推进的场景中。"除了张开嘴,任凭从遥远处传来的词语填满,又能做些什么呢?"

"你觉得我的裙子很傻吗?我觉得……愚蠢……它不太……"

"不,我喜欢,挺好的。"

"我是说,我不太……"

"I would never come to a coffee shop like Soft Filter of my own accord. It's not a Litchi Latte I want. How extremely...tasteless. No, I came there to find *you*...This is so embarrassing to admit but, well, I found you through a video you posted to your blog—the one of you singing that song in your bedroom. And I just knew I had to meet you..."

Though this handsome entertainment industry professional's confession could not have been foreseen based on his past behavior, which in fact would suggest a truth of a completely opposite nature, for Limei, all that he said was logical and unsurprising, having merely the happy effect of confirming the perfect congruence of the two realities, internal and external, whose nonalignment, when in evidence, made the life of Limei so particularly unbearable...

"Perhaps you can tell...that I have a somewhat bulletproof personality. Women are usually attracted to me. Unfortunately, they leave me cold. But I must admit that this singing stirred something deep inside me. So vulnerable—pure—intimate! I felt like I was meeting a total stranger, yet someone I knew deeply at the same time..."

And, even though Limei had always and forever known that he would say this, her heart skipped a beat—right on time.

Kuai continued: "You must have a lot of courage to expose yourself in that way, knowing anyone could see you..."

Now, Limei blushed. Under his eyes, she felt involuntary. The music pressed on her chest. She looked down. Demurely, she twirled the tiny cocktail parasol. She sensed she was inside a scene that would move forward no matter what.

What else was there to do but let her mouth fall open, fill with words put there from far away?

"Do you think my dress is silly? I feel...stupid...it's not very..."

"No, I like it, it's nice."

"I mean, I'm not very..."

"也许你应该靠近一点——这里。"

"如果你觉得……好吧……"

"我们去屋顶吧,好吗?我想**抽烟**。我们可以……在那里多**聊聊**。"

"我觉得……"

"……"

"……"

"上海的夜晚很美,不是吗?看——那边。电视塔。东方明珠。你看到——它在跳动吗?**粉色**的。"

"Maybe you should come closer—here."

"If you think...well...."

"Let's go to the roof, okay? I want to smoke. We can...talk more there."

"I feel..."

"..."

"..."

"The nights in Shanghai are beautiful, don't you think? Look—there. The TV Tower. Oriental Pearl. Do you see—how it's pulsing? Pink."

第十三章: 不打破几颗蛋就做不成蛋饼……

黎美醒来时头痛欲裂。

什么!? 她只喝了一杯酒! 然而,疼痛却如同盲目的橡皮擦在她的大脑中摩擦。此外,她的身体感觉糟透了!

但尤其是…*下面哪里*…

昨晚发生了什么?

她低头看着自己的床单。

上面有一个巨大的污渍……

~ *血!?* ~

黎美的心瞬间冻住。她的眼睛也冻结了。然而,她的脑海却开始狂奔。

黎美在混乱的记忆中寻找。她曾在夜店里。和蒴诗雷交谈,那是肯定的。但是大多数场景似乎都被剪切了! 只有他们对话中的短语不断在她昏暗的脑海中闪现,反复出现,却没有画面或语调,像是缺少舞台指示的剧本……

她呻吟着。这家伙对她做了什么?

哦,天哪! 与蒴诗雷的整个故事竟然变成了最糟糕品味的实验!

而最糟糕的是……她现在必须去见他,签署她的*明星合约*!

Chapter 13: You Have to Break A Few Eggs...

Limei woke with a bad bad headache.

What!? She'd only had one drink! And yet the pain was blinding, rubbing at her brains like an eraser. Plus, her body felt terrible!

But especially... *down there*...

What had happened last night?

She looked down at her sheets.

There was a huge stain of...

~ **Blood!?** ~

The girl's heart froze. Her eyes froze. Her mind, however, started running.

Limei searched her sodden memories. She had been at the nightclub. And she had been talking to Kuai Shilei, that was certain. But most last night's scenes seemed to have been cut! Only phrases from their conversation strobed through her black mind, appearing there again and again without images or intonations, like a script missing stage directions...

She groaned. What had this boy done to her?

Oh, God! This whole story with Kuai Shilei was turning out to be an experiment in the poorest kind of taste imaginable!

And the worst thing was...now she had to go meet him to sign her *talent star contract*!

第十四章: 一个孕育的停顿 (意味深长的停顿)

当电梯"叮"的一声响起时,一位身着粉色波点裙、闪亮雪纺上衣、以及像空乘人员一样紧致发型和举止的女员工,默默地指向开门的方向。黎美顺着她的手指走了出去,踏入了东方明珠旋转餐厅那厚厚的粉色光线中。

东方明珠广播电视塔的设计灵感源自中唐时期一首诗中的一句:"大珠小珠落玉盘。"自助餐厅位于高空之中,就在可口可乐观光层之上,坐落于十五个马卡龙色泡泡中的最上方,沿着卫星塔的银针滑落。

尽管正值正午,夏日阳光在上海上空闪耀,但窗户透出的玫瑰色光泽使得整个空间显得阴暗。被注入这颗泡泡糖般的气泡中,丽梅感到寒冷、迟缓、黏腻。这种通常甜美而可爱的颜色——象征女孩与欢乐的粉色——突然变得令人窒息。粉色也是内里的颜色,而这过于贴近了,过于暴露内里。

游客们在旋转的房间里穿梭,来回搬运着盛满食物的光亮汤碗。圆形的房间呈环状,餐厅的自助餐沿顺时针方向摆放,与餐厅的旋转方向相反。黎美右侧是早餐,左侧是甜点,那里浓厚的人工雾气从堆得高高的水果和冰淇淋碗中戏剧性地倾泻而出。

真奇怪的钟表… 黎美虚弱地想着。即使在这昏暗的粉色光辉中,她的眼睛也感到刺痛。 *我希望能像在自助餐厅里转圈一样轻松地回到过去! 或者至少能快进,跳过这场可怕的会议!*

感觉到雾气在肌肤上游走,黎美的胃在翻腾。她一直讨厌自助餐。

她转过身,朝甜点方向看去,寻找蒯诗雷。

Chapter 14: A Pregnant Pause

When the elevator binged, a feminine employee in the envelope of a pink polka-dotted skirt, shiny chiffon blouse, and the tight hairdo and manner of an airline stewardess pointed silently through the opening doors. Limei followed her finger, stepping into the thick pink light glazing the dining room of the Oriental Pearl Revolving Restaurant.

The design of the Oriental Pearl Radio and Television Tower was inspired by a line in a poem of the Middle Tang period: "big and small pearls falling on a jade plate." The Revolving Restaurant All You Can Eat Buffet was located high in the sky, just above the Coca-Cola Observation Deck, in the topmost of the fifteen magenta spheres impaled on that slide down the silver needle of the satellite tower.

Though it was high noon, and the summer sun shone brightly over Shanghai, the rosy tint of the windows made the space dim, and uniformly pink. Having been injected into this bubblegum bubble, Limei felt cold, slow, sticky. This usually sweet and nice shade—the color of girls and fun—felt, suddenly, claustrophobic. Pink was also the color of insides, and this was too much, too much inside.

Families of tourists shuffled round the circular, spinning room, ferrying plates back and forth between shiny tureens parked with food. The buffet was arranged as a ring, and the meal went clockwise, against the rotation of the restaurant. To Limei's right was breakfast; to her left, dessert, where artificial fog poured dramatically from hedonistically-heaped bowls of fruit and ice cream.

A strange kind of clock...Limei thought weakly. Her eyes hurt, even in the dull pink glow. I wish I could turn back time as easily as walking around this buffet! Or at least fast forward, so I could skip this terrible meeting!

Noticing the fog feeling its way over her skin, Limei's stomach flipped. She had always hated all-you-can-eat buffets.

She turned backwards, towards dessert, looking for Kuai.

第十五章：东方明珠的午餐

在汉堡站对面，隐匿于折叠樱桃木屏风投下的细腻阴影中，黎美的会议如同竹林中的老虎，静静等待着她的到来。

蒯诗雷坐在一张长长的硬木桌旁，身边是一位漂亮、专业的年轻女性。两人都从塑料杯中用吸管喝着汽水。蒯诗雷的眼睛微微半闭，穿着一件紫色的卫衣，拉链是银色的，拉链上有一条白色的线。城市的景色在他身后旋转，逐渐消失在远方。

"下午好，黎美，"蒯诗雷神秘地说道。"你昨晚可能很累。"他指了指他们的汽水。"我也是……可惜这里没有咖啡，只有可乐。"

"我没事……"黎美结结巴巴地回答。

蒯诗雷是在暗指他们昨晚的经历吗？在他的同事面前？！
的。

在意味深长的停顿之后，黎美坐下，瞥了一眼那位女性。她正在整理一叠文件，看起来很中立。她的头发似乎剪得比需要的短，颜色是棕色"我真是酒后不省人事。让我们快点结束，"蒯诗雷说。"我的同事已经准备好了所有资料。这一叠文件包含了你的合同条款：未来付款的规定、保密协议等。请在有箭头的地方签名。"

黎美顺从地签了名。蒯诗雷起身，那个同事也跟着起身。她对黎美微笑，轻轻地触碰了一下蒯诗雷的肩膀。

"这是你的钢笔，"她性感地低声说道。

"谢谢，"蒯诗雷说。他接过钢笔，转过身。

"我们会通知你有项目时的情况。黎美，我们得走了，但请随意享用自助餐，东方玫瑰娱乐公司为你提供的款待。你值得的！"

Chapter 15: Lunch at the Oriental Pearl

Across from the hamburger station, sequestered by discreet shadows cast by folding cherrywood screens, Limei's meeting lay in wait for her like a tiger in a bamboo grove.

Kuai Shilei sat at a long, hard table beside a pretty, professional young woman. Both sucked soda into straws from plastic cups. Kuai's eyes were hooded. He wore a purple sweatshirt. The zipper was silver. The line running up it was white. The city behind him rotated into the distance.

"Good afternoon, Limei," Kuai said inscrutably. "You're probably tired from last night." He gestured at their sodas. "So am I... Unfortunately, they don't have coffee here, only Coca-Cola."

"I'm fine..." Limei stammered.

Was Kuai referencing their night together? Here, in front of his colleague?!

After a pregnant pause, Limei sat down, glancing at the woman. She was straightening a stack of papers. She was very neutral. Her hair seemed shorter than it needed to be. And it was brown.

"Fuck, I am so hungover. Let's make this quick," Kuai said. "My colleague has prepared everything. This stack of paperwork contains the terms of your contract: provisions for future payment, NDA, et cetera. Please sign wherever there's an arrow."

Limei obeyed. Kuai stood up. The colleague stood up. She smiled at Limei. She touched Kuai's shoulder.

"Here's your fountain pen," she whispered sexily.

"Thank you," Kuai said. He took the pen. He spun on his heels.

"We'll let you know when we have a project for you. Limei, we have to be going, but please feel free to enjoy the buffet, with the compliments of Rose Lily Entertainment Company. You deserve it!"

这两位同事毫不犹豫地走进电梯，连看一眼这位有潜力的女星都没有。电梯门"叮"的一声关上，他们快速下行，驶向上海的地面。

黎美走到广播电视塔的边缘，额头紧贴着从地板到天花板的弯曲彩色窗户。她感到恶心。她一直恐高。四周的一切开始扩散和减慢，化为波浪般的粉色光影。空气波，电波——这无形的广播媒介究竟是什么，渗透着里面和外面，万事万物，无处不在？在这个泡泡之外，灰色的城市不断旋转，黎美则高高在上，处于电视塔之顶。许多人生活在那下面，每个人都有自己私密的思想和感受。

黎美突然晕倒在地，静静地躺在旋转餐厅花纹的深红地毯上，直到负责清理盘子的员工过来把她带走。

The two colleagues filed away and into the elevator without a second glance at the talented starlet. The doors dinged closed, and they shot down into Shanghai.

Limei approached the edge of the Radio and Television Tower. She pressed her forehead against the curved, colored windows, which went from floor to ceiling. Limei was still nauseous. She had always been afraid of heights. Everything was spreading and slowing out around her, melting into waves of pink light. Air waves, radio waves—what was it anyways, this invisible broadcast medium, that seeped through insides, outsides, everything, everywhere? Below this bubble, the endless gray city spun by her: little Limei, trapped up on top in her TV tower. Many people lived down there, each with their own private thoughts and feelings.

Limei fainted to the floor, then lay very still on the gigantically maroon carpet of the Revolving Restaurant. She lay there until an employee responsible for clearing away plates came to get her, too.

第十六章: 纯如粉色牛奶

夜店的人群为她的歌声而着迷...

黑暗的房间, 红色的灯光
难道你不想看一张
照片活过来吗?

高脚杯, 小药丸
她想要: 加满
陷阱门, 愉快的刺激
最甜美的致命杀手

她说, 别惊醒
难道你不想看到一
污点变成形状吗?

答案, 空白的空间
但难道你不想在我
的脸上留下一个名字吗?

纯如粉色牛奶
所有的愿望留下痕迹
纯如粉色牛奶
她知道愿望留下痕迹

难道你不想看到一
污点变成形状吗?
难道你不想看到一...

Chapter 16: Pure as Pink Milk

The crowd of the nightclub was spellbound as she sang...

Dark room, red light
Don't you wanna watch a
Photo come to life?

Tall glass, small pill
She wants: refill
Trapdoor, nice thrill
Sweetest sweet kill

She says, don't wake
Don't you wanna see a
Stain become a shape?

Answers, blank space
But don't you wanna put a
Name onto my face?

Pure as pink milk
All wishes leave a trace
Pure as pink milk
She knows wishes leave a trace

Don't you wanna see a
Stain become a shape?
Don't you wanna see a...

PART 3: HYSTERIC GLAMOUR

~ Bruce Lee Proverb ~

"Real living is living for others."
—Bruce Lee

第三部分：歇斯底里的魅力

~ 李小龙箴言 ~

"真实的生活就是为他人而活。"
—李小龙

第十七章: 昏厥沙发 (躺椅)

黎美坐在丝绒沙发上,身后是一位戴眼镜的男人,手里拿着记事本和雪茄。

黎美: 哦, 医生!!! 我最近睡得太差了, 比如说昨晚我梦到自己生活在—

黎美的左拖鞋掉落, 像保龄球般撞击着淡紫色地毯。

黎美: 一间时尚现代的公寓, 所有的一切都是空白的, 我高高在上一座高楼俯瞰着无尽的游乐园, 我坐在窗边, 能看到许多微小的士兵……

她的脚趾甲涂着海贝壳的粉色。医生清了清喉咙。

黎美: 在片场走来走去, 然后我—

另一只拖鞋也砸落在地, 发出轰然巨响。

黎美: 在黑色汽车里被带着游览公园, 五彩纸屑从天而降——

医生急忙站起, 气愤地让雪茄掉落在地毯上。

医生: 好了, 小姐!!! 够了!!!

雪茄在淡紫色地毯上轻轻滚动。

医生: 我在职业生涯中从未听过如此无聊的梦。我再也无法接受你做我的病人了……

雪茄在地毯上来回滚动。

医生: 可怜的女孩。这一切太乏味、太明显、太简单, 没错, 确实是

Chapter 17: Fainting Couch

Limei on a velvet couch; behind her, a bespectacled man with notepad and cigar.

LIMEI: Oh, *doctor*!!! I've been sleeping so poorly, for example, just last night I dreamt I was living—

Limei's left slipper falls off. A bowling-ball sound as it hits the mauve carpet.

LIMEI: alone in a very stylish modern apartment, ALL WHITE EMPTY, I was high up in a TALL TOWER overlooking an endless amusement park, I sat by the WINDOW, I could see many tiny soldiers...

Her toenails: seashell pink. The doctor clears his throat.

LIMEI: walking around on a film set, and then I—

The other slipper crashes to the carpet with a boom.

LIMEI: was being driven around the park in a BLACK CAR and confetti rained down—

The doctor jumps to his feet in exasperation, his cigar falling to the carpet.

DOCTOR: Okay that's enough, Fräulein!!!

It rolls softly back and forth—

DOCTOR: I've never heard such a boring dream in my life...I can simply longer accept you my patient....

Back and forth on the mauve carpet.

DOCTOR: Poor girl. It's all so tedious, obvious, elementary, yes, in fact, yes, no, you are such a clear case...like a textbook....that one wonders whether you even have a subconscious at all!

的,你真是一个典型案例……像教科书一样……令人怀疑你是否真的有潜意识!

黎美流下了眼泪。

医生:我恐怕帮不了你……但啊……是的……也许……

他在记事本上飞快地写下,撕下了一张纸。

医生:我唯一能推荐的办法,我亲爱的,是针灸!

响亮的笑声和掌声。

Limei bursts into tears.

DOCTOR: I'm afraid I cannot help you...But ah...yes...perhaps...

He scribbles furiously in his pad; tears away a sheet of paper.

DOCTOR: The only recourse I can recommend to you, my dear, is acupuncture!

Loud laughter and clapping.

第十八章: 色,戒——别跌倒!

灯光闪烁,先是绿色,接着黄色,最后是红色。可她仍然站在十字路口: 无精打采的黎美。耳塞无力地垂挂在耳边,像枯萎的百合,正在她的脑海中腐烂。

咔擦!!!

黎美惊呼一声,随后感到手掌传来的刺痛感。

"傻瓜,你是在梦游吗? 快让开!"

她怎么会在马路中间双手着地? 更糟糕的是,她的白色运动裙被风吹起,内裤暴露在众人眼前!

像往常一样,黎美**面红耳赤**。

十字路口空无一人,但黎美知道,她并不孤单。她抬头望向旋转的绿树,心中越来越感受到一种蝉鸣般的存在,虽不可见,却真实存在,始终在看着——看着她,看着她的内心,倾听,像她听音乐一样,听着,做出评判,观察,笑着,凝视。

她轻轻抱紧手提包,踉跄着站起身来。

Chapter 18: Lust, Caution—Don't Fall!

The light strobed green, then yellow, then red. And still she stood at the crosswalk: listless Limei. Her earbuds hung limply in her ears, wilted lilies rotting in her mind.

Skrrrrttt!!!

Limei gasped, then felt textured burning in her tender palms.

"Idiot, are you sleepwalking? Get out of the way!"

How had she ended up on her hands and knees, in the middle of the road? To make matters worse, her white sport skirt had flown up in the wind—her underwear was on view for all to see!

As usual, Limei blushed.

The intersection was empty. Still, Limei knew she was not alone. She looked up at the green trees, spinning above. Limei increasingly felt a cicada-like presence, invisible but there, always looking—at her and inside her, looking and listening, like she listened to music, listening, making judgments, watching, laughing, looking.

She clutched her tote bag delicately to her chest as she staggered to her feet.

第十九章：情感戏剧

在软滤镜咖啡馆，黎美的手仍然有些流血，都是她摔倒的结果。但黎美还有其他问题，她面临着三个：

她什么时候能再见到蒴诗雷？
她该说些什么？他又会说些什么？

黎美对这些问题有很多不同的答案，急切地排练着，仿佛在为考试做准备。大多数情况下，她构思着可能发生的可怕事件，降临在他身上。

比如，她可能在咖啡店回家的路上，突然被一辆飞驰而过的红色摩托车撞倒而死。然后，蒴会摘下闪亮的头盔，为自己所做的事而痛哭流涕。

或者，她可能会成名，出现在每个电视脱口秀上。在那里，她会提到一个年轻暴力男子给她带来的不幸。观众会赞扬她的勇气和美德。与此同时，蒴会在夜总会里尽情狂欢。他会无聊地环顾四周，厌倦了派对上那些狂欢的朋友，渴望一个浪漫、敏感、艺术气息浓厚的人，内心丰富。然后，他会低头看自己的手机，看到*她*—盘腿坐在沙发上，搭配着精致的猫跟鞋。泪水、羞愧和渴望涌上他的眼眶。因为，与观众和黎美本人不同，他会知道到底发生了什么。

或者，他可能会在某个晚上打电话给她，说："可爱的黎美，今晚你在哪里？"她会回答："我当然在家，准备睡觉，编辫子。你竟敢打电话给我？"

黎美创作了许多这种场景的变体，但它们的效果都是一样的。尽管这些事件虽然不太可能，但在技术上却是可行的，仍然总能让她泪流满面。这些泪水不受控制地滴入她的拿铁中，为每一杯增添了一丝时尚的海盐风味。

Chapter 19: Melodrama

At Soft Filter, Limei's hands were still feeling cherry-red from her fall. But this young barista had other problems. The top three:

When would she see Kuai Shilei again?
What would she say? What would he say?

Limei had many different answers to these questions, all of which she rehearsed urgently, as though preparing for exams. Mostly, she drafted terrible events that could befall him.

For example, she might be walking home from the coffee shop, only to be run over and killed by a speeding red motorcycle. Then Kuai would tear away his shining helmet and weep in regret for what he'd done.

Or she might become famous and be on every TV talk show. There, she would reference a misfortune that had been done to her by a violent young man. The audience would praise her courage and virtue. Kuai, meanwhile, would be reveling at the nightclub. He would look around in boredom, tired of his party animal friends and wishing for a romantic, sensitive, artistic person with a rich inner life. Then he would look down at his phone and see *her*—cross-legged, kitten heels tucked neatly beneath her. Tears, shame, and desire would come to his eyes. For, unlike the audience and unlike Limei herself, he would know exactly what had happened.

Or he might call her one night and say, "Lovely Limei, where are you tonight?" and she would say "I'm at home, of course, dressing for bed and braiding my hair. How dare you call me?"

Limei created many variations on these scenes, but their effects were all the same. Unlikely though technically possible, they never failed to bring tears to her eyes. These fell unchecked into her lattes, flavoring each with a trendy taste of sea salt.

第二十章: 针灸

洁白的医生办公室,流水的声音轻柔悦耳。黎美躺在检查台上,皱巴巴的纸巾覆盖着。

医生: 我能看出有什么事情困扰着你。让我来帮你。请换上这个,然后趴在桌子上。

医生消失了。
黎美脱掉了所有衣服。
她赤裸着身体。她感到一阵寒意。
她穿上了印花纸质袍子。
她躺下。医生再次出现。

医生: 很好……我将在这里、这里和这里扎针。别担心,这很传统。现在让我来解开你背后的绑带……

他俯下身,双手搓揉着。

他惊恐地后退。

医生: 哦,我的天!!!我一生中从未见过这样的情况!!!我的亲爱的……你怎么会……完全没有脊椎呢?为什么……你简直就是个无脊椎动物!!!

观众发出惊叹声和大笑。

Chapter 20: Acupuncture

Clean white doctor's office, soothing sound of running water.
Limei on the crinkly tissue covering the examination table.

DOCTOR: I can see something is bothering you. Let me help you. Please change into this thing here and lie face down on the table.

The doctor disappears.
Limei takes off all her clothes.
She is naked. She shivers.
She puts on the paper gown.
She lies down. The doctor reappears.

DOCTOR: Good...I'm going to stick needles HERE, HERE, and HERE. Don't worry, this is very traditional. Now allow me to undo these ties in the back...

He leans over her, rubbing his hands together...

He recoils in horror.

DOCTOR: Oh my god!!! I've never seen this before in my life!!! My dear...how is it that...you have no back bone at all? Why...you're completely spineless!!!

Gasps and loud laughter.

第二十一章：最残酷的评论

"喂？*喂？*"有人在叫嚷。"请来一杯浪漫薰衣草玫瑰惊喜拿铁。"

"哎呀……抱歉……"

当她终于将这杯饮品放到面前时，她感到经理的呼吸像微波炉一样在她脖子后面加热。

"黎美！"经理低声道。"这应该是一杯浪漫薰衣草玫瑰惊喜拿铁吗？看看你做的！这根本不是玫瑰，它是……它是……我真不知道该怎么说！立刻重做，但要更好！"

黎美羞愧地低下头。她经理说得没错，黎美在柔软的白色泡沫上画的不是绽放的玫瑰，而是一个眼窝里爬满虫子的骷髅。

"而且不要再迟到了，知道吗？否则，我不得不解雇你。这周已经第二次了！"

"我很抱歉，我很抱歉！我早上总是感觉……不舒服……"

当她重新开始制作咖啡时，身后同事们的嘲笑声不断传来，更加让她感到羞辱。

"你看到没有？她差点又把牛奶洒！"

"她怎么总是看起来那么疲惫？"

"她说自己睡不好，但我觉得*另有原因*……"

"没错——她表现得很无辜，但那个女孩的内心就像一本露骨的小说！"

"她是在哭吗？"

Chapter 21: The Cruelest Comments

"Hello? *Hello?*" Someone had barked. "One lukewarm Romance Lavender Rose Surprising Latte, please."

"Oops...Sorry..."

When she finally set this drink before her, she felt the breath of her boss microwaving the back of her neck.

"Limei!" her manager hissed. "Is that supposed to be a Romance Lavender Rose Surprising Latte? Look what you've done! This is no rose, it's...It's...I don't know what to say! Repeat it immediately, but better!"

Limei looked down in shame. What her boss said was true. Instead of an unfurling flower, Limei had painted a skull with worms inside eye sockets in the soft white foam.

"And don't be late again, okay? Otherwise, I'll have to let you go. This is the second time this week!"

"I'm sorry, I'm sorry! I've been feeling so...sick in the morning..."

As she started the coffee over again, she heard the voices of her fellow baristas twittering in the background, further abusing and humiliating her.

"Did you see? She almost dropped the milk again!"

"Why does she look so tired all the time?"

"She says she has trouble sleeping, but I think it's *something else...*"

"You're right—she acts innocent, but that girl is easy to read as a very graphic novel!"

"Look—is she crying? I can't tell..."

第二十二章: 原声带

当黎美走在回家的路上,她的思绪像早晨的红绿灯一样闪烁。然而,始终是同样的颜色,一遍又一遍:红、红、红。

小心点,女孩……生活中有一样东西是你永远无法找回的! 黎美曾在每本书、每部电影、每个母亲的嘴里听到过这样的话。然而,她却像是在*超市*里买*牛奶*一样,轻易地放弃了自己的*纯真*,以为明天还能*再*买回来!

但实际上,黎美根本不在乎她妈妈的想法……她只是在夸张罢了!

她戴上耳机: 说谎的黎美,令人厌恶的黎美。她听着歌词,然后更多的歌词。这些歌词伴随着她的步伐,讲述着一段可怕的爱情。她扯掉了耳机。

…我正在编辫子。你怎么敢给我打电话?

然后,她停住了。

黎美是被脚步声和沉重的呼吸声跟着吗?

但当她小心翼翼地回头看时,她是孤单一人。只有蝉声: 虽然她看不见它们,但她知道它们就在那儿。

哦,天哪,外面的世界就像是我内心状态的完美象征! 黎美痛苦地想。

黎美知道象征的意思: 不真实。但她无能为力——她快速地跑回了家。当她推开心门并将其锁上时,径直走向邻里的警察。

Chapter 22: Soundtrack

As Limei walked home, her thoughts blinked at her like that morning's stoplights. But it was always the same color, over and over again: red, red, red.

Be careful, little girl...There's one thing in life you can never get back! How many times had Limei heard such words—in every book, every movie, every mother's mouth? And yet she had given away her *purity* as though it were a carton of *milk* that she could just buy *again* the next *day* at the *grocery store*!

But actually, Limei didn't care what her mother thought at all.... She was just being dramatic!

She put on her headphones: lying Limei, loathsome Limei. She listened to lyrics, then more lyrics. The lyrics walked her steps, telling her of a terrible love. She tore off her headphones.

...braiding my hair. How dare you call me?

Then, she stopped.

Was Limei being followed by footsteps? And heavy breathing?

But when she cast one cautious eye behind her, she was alone. Only the sound of cicadas.

Oh god, the outside is like an exact symbol of my mental state! Limei thought miserably.

Limei did know what a symbol was: not real. But she couldn't help it—she ran quickly all the way home. When she pushed through the heart-gate and clasped it closed, she went right up to the neighborhood policeman in his booth.

"警官,警官!有人在跟踪我!"她紧张地说。"请锁上这个门!"

他回头看了看她身后的黑暗。

"嗯……好吧……"他慢慢地说。

"Sir, sir! Someone's following me!" she said nervously. "Please lock this gate!"

He looked behind her, at the darkness.

"Hm...alright..." he said slowly.

第二十三章: 她的最后一杯拿铁

你被解雇了!"

这句话响亮地关上了大门。

哦,不...

黎美将工作服挂起来,周围传来一阵大笑。

Chapter 23: Her Last Latte

"You're fired!"

The words clanged loudly shut.

Oh no...

Limei hung up her work costume to a large audience of laughter.

第二十四章: 迷失在深渊中

在黎美的房间里,她的吉他孤零零地放在角落,干枯得像个木偶,连泪水都没有落在上面。

如今,丽梅已经不再玩乐,她只是在重播与反思。

她的第一首歌曾带来最纯粹的美好感觉。这首歌,她甚至一开始都不想让别人听到! 然而,还是有人听到了。而接下来发生的事情却糟糕透顶。那种感觉,再也无法重现了。第一次,总归只有一次。

看着笔记本电脑,黎美重播了几个月前发布的视频。屏幕上,黎美的脸被蓝光照亮。她对着镜头微笑。

更糟糕的是,她的第二次也未曾发生。丽梅试了很多次,想再唱出一首新曲。但她的嘴仿佛只会唱一首歌。一首歌,一个固定的旋律,总在脑海中回荡。虽然歌词可以随意更换、伪装,但旋律却深深扎根。尽管现在一切都变得不同,也更糟,但似乎没有任何新的东西诞生; 她依然如故,总是原来的模样。对于丽梅的生命来说,再没有其他歌词可写。

"大家好!"黎美说道。"好吧……严格来说,没人……哈哈。显而易见。但我不介意……好了,无论如何,这是我写的第一首真正的歌,算是……"

然后黎美弹着她的大吉他,唱起了《桃花皮之夜》。

黎美是可爱的,简单而天真。对蒴诗雷来说,她或许就像一块可食用的**卡通可颂**。想到这里,一阵寒意划过她的脊背。

此时的歌,黎美听来同样纯真。虽然有些音调和歌词不好,但她听着自己犯的错误,眼泪不禁夺眶而出,这些错误再也无法第一次去犯.

Chapter 24: Mise en Abîme

Limei's guitar sat in the corner, sad and dry, like a wooden doll. Not even teardrops fell upon it.

These days, Limei did not play, she replayed and reflected.

Her first song had been the best good feeling. This first song...she had not even wanted anyone to hear it!!...But someone had. And what happened next was bad and terrible. Now, she would never have this feeling ever again. A first time does not happen twice.

Looking at her laptop, Limei pressed replay on the video she had posted only mere months ago. On the screen, Limei's face lifted itself, and was lit blue. Limei smiled into the camera.

The worse thing was, her second time would not happen, either. Limei had tried many times to sing again, a new tune. But her mouth seemed to know only one song. One song, one shape, echoing always. Words might come and go, she could switch and fake them, but her melody—this, she could not get out of her head. Although everything, now, was different and worse, it seemed that nothing at all was new; she was always identical as ever before, and there were no other lyrics possible for the life of Limei.

"Hi everyone!" Limei said. "Well...technically no one...haha. Obviously. But I don't mind...Okay, anyways, this is my first real song I've written, kind of..."

Then Limei sang "Peach Skin Nights" while strumming her big guitar.

Limei was cute, yes...simple and naive. To Kuai Shilei perhaps she had appeared as a **cartoon croissant**: edible. (At this thought, a shiver was sent down her spine!)

The song, Limei heard now, was also innocent. There were wrong notes and bad words. And yet tears fell from her eyes at the sound of the mistakes she would never make for the first time again.

好吧，如果她再唱一首新歌，*绝对*不会让任何人听到！！

而且，如果她曾以那种敏感的歌声吸引了蒯的注意，也许她还可以再试一次……

黎美重播了视频。

"大家好！"她说。"好吧……严格来说，没人……哈哈。显而易见。但我不介意……我想我就是喜欢唱歌……好了，无论如何，这是我写的第一首真正的歌，算是……"

黎美随着黎美的声音口型一致地唱。她的表情也在同样变化。黎美朝镜头微笑，黎美眯起眼睛。她越看黎美，越觉得黎美似乎不那么真实……对黎美来说，她似乎是个陌生人。难道黎美一直在想象自己？

那张床、那张床的皱褶，从笔记本电脑内部延伸到外部；墙上的照片在她眼前回旋；她那双小手依旧如初。

当黎美唱着《桃花皮之夜》，她听着黎美逐渐走向自我深渊的边缘，那条深埋在她胸膛中的隧道，仿佛一个洞，然而并非真正的洞，因为它并未打开，反而像一条莫比乌斯带，稀有而有趣，却最终只是一个被压扁的洞，环绕着，完美地封闭着，但在她体内——黎美明白，这意味着她是空心的。

拥有这样的空洞并不好。这并不好，但确实非常诱人。那条无尽的道路似乎没有尽头，因此，偶尔回忆起内心的无限符号形状的人行道，走在上面，听着歌词，独自前行，歌词在聆听她，陪伴着她，独自漫步。

但不，这并不好，黎美一直都知道。许多她喜欢的东西都是这样的：不好的。

也许，悲伤就是她永恒的最爱。大多数孩子随着成长和成年的过程

Well, she thought, if she ever did sing a new song, she would *never* let anyone hear it!!

Besides, if she had caught Kuai's attention with her sensitive singing one time, maybe she could do it again...

Limei replayed the video.

"Hi everyone!" she said. "Well...technically no one...haha. Obviously. But I don't mind...I guess I just like singing...Okay, anyways, this is my first real song I've written, kind of..."

Limei mouthed the words in time to Limei. She moved her face in the same way, too. Limei smiled into the camera and Limei narrowed her eyes. The more Limei watched her, the less convincing the young girl seemed. Had Limei been imagining herself the whole time?

There and there was the same bed, continuously crumpled from inside to outside the laptop, there and there were the photos on the wall behind her and on the wall in front of her, and there were her same small hands.

As Limei sang "Peach Skin Nights," she listened to Limei walking further and further along the edges of the abyss of herself that had always tunneled through her chest, like a hole, except not really a hole because it was not open, instead like a Möbius strip, a rare and interesting figure, maybe, but ultimately just a hole, a flattened hole that went around and around and was perfectly closed, but inside her—which, Limei understood, meant she was hollow.

It was not good to have this kind of hole. It was not good, but because its path could never end, it had been at times comforting to remember this ribboning, infinity sign-shaped sidewalk inside herself along which her mind could walk forever, listening to lyrics, walking alone, lyrics listening to her, lyrics walking her along, alone.

But no, it was not good, she had always known. Many things Limei liked were like this: not good.

Maybe sadness was just her favorite food, forever. Most children change their tastes as they grow older and become adults. They

改变他们的口味。他们喜欢糖果,然后后来喜欢健康的食物。但一些人,黎美此刻意识到,永远保持着孩子的心态,味蕾永远不会盛开,他们也不会。像孩子一样,这些人热爱脆弱,而这正是黎美自己所厌恶的特质。

黎美戴上她笨重的耳机。她将双膝抱紧,裹着的小脚丫在粉色的床上留下了两个小小的印记。她轻轻低下下巴,望向窗外。雨水在城市上空倾泻,垂直的灰色划痕。轻音乐中的黎美。

她剥开了桃子包,撕掉粘人的保鲜膜,再揭开湿润的纸,纸下的包子软得像个玩具,而不太像食物。

黎美吃着她的长生桃包,它的味道和往常一样。只是之前,她从未意识到,实际上,桃子包已经像桃乌龙马提尼一样美味。

like candy, and then later, they like things that are good for them. But some people, Limei realized now, stayed children forever, and their tastebuds never flowered, and they didn't, either. Like children, such people loved weakness, a quality Limei, like herself, despised.

Limei put on her clunky headphones. She drew her knees in to her chest. Her small feet, with small socks on them, made two small impressions in the pink bed. She dropped her chin neatly and looked out the window. Rain fell on the city, vertical dashes, dark gray. Lo-fi Limei.

She unwrapped her peach bun, peeling away the sticky clingfilm, then the damp paper adhering to the underside of the bun, which was soft like a stuffed animal, and not much like food.

Limei ate her live-forever infinity peach bun, and it tasted like just like it always had. Only before, she hadn't known that really, a peach bun had already tasted like a Peach Oolong Martini.

PART 4: GOOD GIRL GONE BAD

~ Third Confucian Proverb ~

> *"You cannot open a book without learning something."*
> —*Confucius*

第四部分: 乖女孩变坏

~ 第三句孔子箴言 ~

> *"开卷有益。"*
> —孔子

第二十五章: 无牵无挂

在中国玫瑰大酒店私人夜总会,黎美每次都像贴纸一样微笑。这就像是小女孩在电影院里,在灯光熄灭、演出开始之前的期待时刻——但其实并不是,因为黎美已经看过这部电影一百万次了。

她凝视着灯光,凝视着空荡荡的观众席。

"接下来我们有……*《桃肤之夜》*!"艾迪带着一丝油腻的声音调侃道。

于是,熟悉的旋律响起……

Chapter 25: No Strings Attached

At China Rose Paramount Private Nightclub, Limei smiled each time like a sticker. It was like being a little girl in the movie theater, after the lights had come down and before everything began—except not really, because Limei had already seen this movie one million times.

She looked into the light. She looked into the empty audience.

"And next we have... *Peach Skin Nights*!" Eddy crooned sleazily.

And so the familiar melody began...

第二十六章: 鸽子的初次飞翔

你好啊, 曾经的我
心在云端, 纯真又美丽
孤身生活, 无法理解
当然我会害羞, 当你握住我的手

碗里的樱桃滴落樱桃色
樱桃在你眼中深深渗透
而你的袖子, 毫无污渍
只有我的声音暴露我的羞耻

梦中的影子在变幻
叹息化为一声尖叫
黑色的墨水与奶油混合

在我心中洒下了一点
我再也无法逃离
我低声呢喃, 但其实我
希望我能大声呼喊...

请转身, 让我一个人待着
像我这样的女孩无处可逃
这里没有人能倾听我的恳求
你走了, 我只需要一件事...

一块香皂, 让我重归洁白
带我回到鸽子的第一次飞行, 再一次
一块香皂, 让我重焕光彩
去除夜晚的气息, 再一次

他们说时间只能向前走
但我跪在地上, 被迫祈祷
希望历史能修复这块破碎的翡翠
洗净你留下的污垢

一块香皂, 让我重归洁白
带我回到鸽子的第一次飞行, 再一次
再一次, 再一次...

Chapter 26: Dove's First Flight

Hello there, girl I used to be
Head in the clouds, pure and pretty
Alone in a life I didn't understand
So of course I was shy, when you took my hand

Cherries in a dish leak cherry dye
Cherries bleeding red deep in your eye
And yet your sleeves, no signs of stain
Only my voice reveals my shame

A shifting shadow from my dream
A sigh that turned into a scream
Blackest ink mixed in with cream

Spilled a spot in my mind
I never can get out
I whisper but really I
Wish I'd thought to shout...

Turn away, please just let me be
There's nowhere left a girl like me can flee
And there's no one here whose heart will hear my plea
Now you're gone there's just one thing I need...

A soap, soap to make me white again
Take me back to a dove's first flight, again
A soap, soap to make me bright again
To take away the smell of night again

They say time only goes one way
But on my knees I'm forced to pray
That history will heal this broken jade
And rinse me of the mess you made

A soap, soap to make me white again
Take me back to a dove's first flight, again
Again, again, again...

第二十七章：完美蓝

然后她从光中走出，回到她的生活。

当她再次融入她来的黑色天鹅绒帷幕时，擦去了唇膏上冷金属麦克风的味道。

她转身，走进那条有花纹的走廊。

在走廊里，一个男人挡住了她的去路。他的眼镜反射着光——从哪里来的？

看着这两个平坦的圆圈，她可以感觉到他是一个非常重要的人物。

"有什么我可以帮忙的吗？"她问。

Chapter 27: Perfect Blue

Then she dropped away from the light, and back to her life.

As she melted once more into the black velvet curtain from which she'd come, Limei wiped the taste of the cold metal microphone from the lacquer of her lipstick.

Now, she turned herself backwards, into the patterned hallway.

Here, a man was blocking her path. His glasses reflected light—from where?

Looking at these two flat circles, she could tell he was a very important person.

"Can I help you?" she said.

第二十八章：红晕反应

黄昏的微光洒在房间里。一只猫头鹰悄无声息地从一端飞到另一端。角落里有一个戴眼镜的男人，长桌对面坐着另一个男人，而第一个男人的助手是——丽梅，职业化装扮，妆容齐整，端坐在一大堆文件和各种设备后面。这些设备全都指向她。桌子上堆满了文书和各种设备。第二位男士解释说这些设备是在评估她。

当他调整一个小圆形摄像头的位置时，目光跟随着她的香烟，从空气中滑向她的嘴唇……

黎美：你介意我**抽烟**吗？

男人：这不会影响测试。

他回头看着面前的屏幕，屏幕上是她的瞳孔，放大并在画面中剧烈移动。

随着黎美被问到一系列强烈、深入、私人的问题，像是在试镜一样，她努力地尝试用真实的方式回答……

Chapter 28: Blush Response

Yellow twilight; an owl; a big, fancy room. There is one bespectacled man in the corner, and one man across the long, dark table, and the assistant of the first man is: Limei, professional, in full costume and makeup, sat cross-legged behind a large pile of paperwork and a lot of equipment, all pointed right at her.

Displayed on the screens facing the second man are her pupils, magnified and shifting enormously in the frame. As he corrects the position of a small circular camera, his eyes follow the glow of her cigarette as it moves from the air to her mouth...

LIMEI: Do you mind if I smoke?

MAN: It won't affect the test.

And as Limei responds realistically to a series of intense and personal questions, clicking and measuring sounds begin to sparkle up and down the table...

第二十九章: 珍珠牡丹

"很不错的裙子,"他说。

黎美越过那名男子的肩膀,望向门口,望向微微叮当作响的薰衣草流苏,望向她把东西存放在小金属储物柜里的房间。

她回过头,看到黑色天鹅绒帷幕轻轻摇曳,走廊在她身边收缩。

"抱歉,我要回更衣室了……"

心跳加速,她向左侧迈了一步,却被他的右手紧紧箍住了腰间。

"嘿,别走。"

"我不想吓到你,"他这次语气更温柔。

"我只是想给你我的名片。你是位非常有才华的表演者。我在一家叫珍珠牡丹娱乐公司的机构工作。随时给我们打个电话。"

Chapter 29: Pearl Peony

"Very nice dress," he said.

Limei looked past the man, towards the door, towards the lavender fringe tinkling silently, towards the room where she stored her things in a small metal locker.

She looked behind her, at the black velvet curtain rippling softly. The hallway's pattern closed around her.

"Excuse me, I'm just heading back to the changing room..."

Heart racing, she stepped to the left, only to be met by his right hand—cinched tightly around the small of her waist.

"Hey, don't go."

"I don't want to scare you," he said, more softly now.

"I just wanted to give you my business card. You're a very talented performer. I work for an agency called Pearl Peony Entertainment Company. Just...give us a call some time."

第三十章: 蒙太奇

"鸽子的初次飞翔"伴随着一系列历史镜头的拼贴播放……

黎美身穿花卉旗袍，走在林荫大道上。她转过身，露出微笑。红润的脸颊在日历的插图中显现。马提尼酒: 在和平饭店的国际社交场。1935年: 女孩们欢笑着跳入泳池。一位女学生走在街上。一辆人力车停下—一只小猫追着一团毛线。帷幕拉开。手在钢琴上滑动。日本巡洋舰悄然沿河而上。飞扬的彩旗: 赛马场上的热闹日子。树荫下有柠檬水。黎美在舞台上轻轻摇摆。1927年: 阮玲玉举起一杯可口可乐。她举起一片拜耳阿司匹林。一只酒壶被塞进了吊袜带。沟渠里清理着机枪。一位女性被拉进出租车。1937年: 炸弹在南京路上空投下。葬礼队伍延绵三英里。三人因灵感过度而猝死。在一张古董梳妆台前，黎美把脸浸入瓷盆的水中。乌云铺天盖地，暗灰色的天空降临。成群的鸽子冲向一块白色肥皂。雨落下，肥皂被浸湿。手指轻柔地握住肥皂，轻轻揉搓。黎美从笑脸上冲洗掉泡沫。玫瑰在延时拍摄中绽放，大小珍珠落在翡翠盘上，泰迪熊、哭泣的小猫、红色毛线、粉色泡泡、迪斯科球、完美的肌肤、闪亮的眼睛、鸽子翱翔在婴儿蓝的天空中：" 鸽子的传统—为了更清新的未来。青春永不衰老。"

Chapter 30: Montage

"Dove's First Flight" plays over a collage of historical footage...

Limei, floral qipao, walks a tree-lined boulevard. She turns and smiles. Rosy cheeks appear on a calendar pinup. Martinis: the international set at the Peace Hotel. 1935: girls laugh and dive into the pool. A schoolgirl walks down the street. A pedicab stops—a kitten chases after a ball of yarn. A curtain opens. Hands run over a piano. Cruisers creep upriver. Flying colors: a day at the racetrack. There is lemonade in the shade. There is Limei on stage, swaying softly. 1927: Ruan Lingyu holds up a glass of Coca-Cola. She holds up a tablet of Bayer Aspirin. A flask is being tucked into a garter. A machine gun is being cleaned in the gutter. A woman is being pulled into a taxi. 1937: bombs over Nanking Road. At an antique vanity, Limei plunges her face into the water of a porcelain basin. The clouds open onto a dark gray sky. A flurry of doves bursts into a white bar of soap. Rain falls—the soap is wet—fingers rub it slowly, and Limei rinses bubbles from her laughing face. Roses blooming in time lapse, big and small pearls falling on a jade plate, a teddy bear, crying kitten, red yarn, perfect skin, shiny eye, doves soaring out in to a baby blue sky. This is "THE TRADITION OF DOVE—FOR A FRESHER FUTURE. YOUTH NEVER GETS OLD."

第三十一章: 电视特别节目

一个旋转的标志；轻快的音乐；电视演播室。吸引人的裸砖墙；大型落地窗外是夜晚的天际线；黎美；一张米色沙发；一位戴眼镜的主持人。

主持人：大家晚上好，上海。刚才播放的那段模糊视频剪辑是新晋明星黄黎美在她卧室录制并发布到个人博客上的迷人歌曲《鸽子的第一次飞翔》的早期版本。我想你们一定会认出这首歌，这周在"病毒"香皂广告中使用的正是这首歌——你们都知道那则广告！如果你和我一样，整个星期都在哼着这曲调。这则广告因其独特而艺术的美学而备受赞誉，结合了"复古"的创意概念与崭新的声音——还有面孔！

我非常高兴今晚在演播室里有年轻的黎美小姐。让我们为她热烈鼓掌吧！

黎美微笑着，礼貌地低下头。

主持人：首先，我想向观众展示我们记者本周拍摄的一些画面：

外景：软滤咖啡店。顾客排队绕过街区。
内景：顾客争先恐后地下单。黎美在柜台后面，一杯接一杯地制作拿铁。

主持人：我从未见过如此受欢迎的咖啡师！黎美，你从一个简单的咖啡店女孩一夜之间变成了全国轰动的明星。很多人都说，广告的成功源于你歌词中真实而深刻的情感。请问我说得对吗，你是自己写这首歌的吗？

黎美：是的，我是。我常常一个人在卧室里写歌唱歌。我真的没想到会有这么多人听到它！

主持人：哇——她真谦虚，大家。黎美，这是一首如此动人、悲伤的

Chapter 31: TV Special

A rotating logo; an upbeat jingle; a TV studio. Attractive exposed-brick walls; the night skyline in large bay windows; Limei; a beige couch; a bespectacled TV presenter.

INTERVIEWER: Good evening Shanghai. That grainy video clip you just saw was an early version of breakout star Huang Limei's enchanting song "Dove's First Flight," recorded in her bedroom and posted to her personal blog. I think you'll recognize the tune from this week's "viral" soap commercial—you know the one! If you're anything like me, you've been humming along all week. The commercial has been praised for its unique and artistic aesthetic, combining a "vintage" creative concept with a fresh new voice—and face!

I'm very pleased to announce that in the studio with me tonight is young Miss Limei herself. Let's have a round of applause!

Limei smiles and ducks her head politely.

INTERVIEWER: First off, I want to show the viewers some footage our reporters took this week:

Ext: Soft Filter coffee. A line wraps around the block.
Int: Customers clamoring to order. Limei, behind counter, serving latte after latte.

INTERVIEWER: I've never seen such a popular barista! Limei, you went from simple girl working at a coffee shop to national sensation over night. Many say the popularity of the commercial is due to the authenticity of your voice and feelings shining through the lyrics. Am I correct in saying that you wrote the song yourself?

LIMEI: Yes, I did. I do a lot of writing and singing just for myself, alone in my bedroom. I had no idea it would end up being heard by so many people!

INTERVIEWER: Wow—she's so modest, everyone. Limei, this is

歌曲。灵感来自哪里呢?

黎美:嗯......我不想详细讲...

主持人:当然,我不是想打扰你。

黎美:不过,我可以说这首歌是受到一些非常痛苦的记忆的启发。我写这首歌部分是为了警告像我这样的女孩,不要犯类似的错误。

主持人:我明白了。这个信息真是跨时代的,尤其对年轻人来说,今天听到这样的内容是多么重要。广告的历史视角是不是也想表达这个?

黎美:嗯,当然我不是广告的策划者......这一切都要归功于Dove优秀的团队。但我觉得,这则广告不仅仅是关于香皂,它也是关于过去的痛苦......也许是从过去吸取教训,同时又将其洗去......好吧......我想......它是关于展望更光明的未来......

主持人:我明白了......那么,黎美,你接下来有什么计划呢?

such a moving, sad song. Where did the inspiration come from for you?

LIMEI: Well...I don't want to go into the particulars...

INTERVIEWER: Of course, I don't mean to pry.

LIMEI: However, I will say that it was inspired by some very painful memories. I wrote the song in part to warn girls like myself from making similar mistakes.

INTERVIEWER: I see. Well it's truly a timeless message, though perhaps especially important for young people to hear today. Is that what the historical perspective of the commercial is looking to express?

LIMEI: Well, I wasn't behind the commercial of course...This is all due to the really great team at Dove. But yes, I think the advertisement is not just about soap, it is—there is a clear message, yes...a tale as old as time... I think, well, I would say it is about— new and old!

INTERVIEWER: I see...In that case, what's next for you, Limei?

第三十二章：炒蛋

幸运的黎美走下拍摄现场，带着每一台在中国各地打开的电视所散发的光芒。

"你太棒了，"她的采访者说道，眼镜片闪烁得厉害。"希望能看到你更多的身影！"

当她腼腆地在柔软的地毯上走过时，所有人都像快乐的相机一样对这个浪漫、敏感、艺术气息满满的年轻女孩微笑。

一束花被递到她的怀里；她接过它们。这些花如此昂贵，她从未见过它们的形状。它们美丽得令人惊叹！

"这些是谁送的？"黎美问那位恭敬、像鞠躬一样的助理，她急匆匆地陪着她走过走廊。

"我相信是蒯先生？"她向着宽广而充满活力的媒体工作室入口挥了挥手。"他一直在这里等你！"

果然，蒯诗雷懒散地靠着墙。

黎美立刻停下了脚步。

她已经等了这个时刻九个月，但现在，她再也不知道接下来会发生什么。

她向左侧一步，却被他的右手紧紧环住了小腰。

"嘿，别走。"他漫不经心地说。

"我只是想告诉你一件事，"他现在语气柔和。

"是……是吗？"她结结巴巴。

Chapter 32: Scrambled Eggs

Lucky Limei stepped off the set carrying the glow of every TV that she turned on all across China.

"You were wonderful," her interviewer said, twinkling his spectacles furiously. "I hope I'll be seeing more of you!"

Everyone smiled like happy cameras at this romantic, sensitive, and artistic young girl as she glided shyly across what felt to her like cream of carpet.

A bouquet thrust into her opened arms; she received it. Here were flowers so expensive she had never seen their shapes before....They were beautiful!

"Who are these from?" Limei asked the respectful, bow-like assistant, as she accompanied her hurriedly down the halls.

"A Mr. Kuai, I believe was his name?" she waved towards the entrance to the vast and dynamic media studio complex. "He's been waiting here for you!"

In fact, there was Kuai Shilei, leaning rakishly.

Limei stopped still.

She had been waiting for this moment for nine months, but now, she no longer knew what was going to happen.

She stepped to the left, only to be met by his right hand—cinched tightly around the small of her waist.

"Hey, don't go," he said casually.

"I just wanted to tell you something," he said now, more softly.

"那则广告真的很棒。如此灵感……而你表现得太出色了,具有磁性。"

"哦,嗯……"黎美支支吾吾,露出微笑。"我不知道。这只是一则香皂广告。我不是个真正的歌手,也不是个真正的演员。"

"不是,不是,当然不是。"蒯挥了挥手。"但这更好!我看到你那个卧室流行视频时就知道你特别——对了,我很抱歉,最近一些项目进展慢,作为新人有些失误——但……总之。那首歌,叫什么来着……'桃子'……虽然有些潜力,但也不尽如人意,你不觉得吗?有点业余的美感。这首歌更成熟。再加上,你那种独立的风格……总是甜美微笑……我不知道……但是这个,我喜欢。乖女孩变坏,这更合适。就像蕾哈娜。把这些元素放进广告里——真聪明。"只有我的声音揭示我的羞愧"?对于鸽子香皂来说,这可真黑暗,哈哈。加入政治角度,那些战争的内容,聪明,聪明……还有艺术指导……拼贴美学……哇,太后现代了!你知道'后现代'吗?对了,不,你可能像十二岁一样,哈哈。所以后现代主义就是……

"Y-yes?" she stammered.

"That commercial really was great. So inspired...and you were amazing. Magnetic!"

"Oh, well..." Limei mumbled, smiling. "I don't know. It's just a soap commercial. I'm not a real singer. Or a real actress."

"No, no, of course not," Kuai said, waving his hand. "But this is way better! I knew you were special when I saw that bedroom pop video—and I'm sorry, by the way, I know I've dropped the ball a bit, projects have been slow recently for debut talent—but... Anyways. That first song, what was it called..."Peaches"...it was promising, but not quite there, don't you think? Kind of had an amateur aesthetic. This is much more polished. Plus, I mean, you with the whole indie thing...The smiling...Smiling sweetly all the time...I don't know...But this, I like. Good girl gone bad, it works much better. And the idea of putting this stuff in a commercial— brilliant. 'Only my voice reveals my shame'? Pretty dark for Dove Soap, haha. Adding the political angle, that war stuff, is smart, smart...And the art direction...the collage aesthetic...wow, how postmodern! Do you know 'postmodern'? Right, no, you're like twelve haha. So postmodernism is like when..."

第三十三章：沉默的星星

黎美以为自己的心已经被打碎过……现在，她听到它再次破裂。她越过蒯的肩膀，看向打开的门，朝着更衣室镜子里映出的自己。她看着他的脸，看着这两张脸，却都无法理解。越是他盯着她的左眼、右眼说话，黎美就越觉得他似乎根本无法真正看见自己。她在哪里？于是，她盯着这颗沉默的明星的脸：栩栩如生的丽梅。鼻子，嘴唇，颧骨。她注视着，等待那些即将出现的词语，为这一场景赋予最终的意义。

一台电视打开，接着另一台，再到另一台……

Chapter 33: Silent Star

Limei thought her heart had already been broken before... Well, there was a second time for everything. She looked past Kuai, towards the open door, towards her face, framed in the changing room mirror. She looked at his face. She looked at both these faces, and she could not understand. The longer he spoke to her, looking in her left eye, looking in her right eye, the more she knew that the real Limei was nowhere to be seen. Where was she? So she watched the face of this silent star: lifelike Limei. Nose, lips, cheekbones. She watched and waited for the words that would soon appear to give a final meaning to this scene.

One TV turned on, then another, then another...

第三十四章: 对话

"你为什么就不能让我一个人静一静！？"

"你是什么意思，黎美？我想祝贺你……我是认真的，这真太棒了！我只希望我能第一个这样做！珍珠牡丹，哎……但是……我不明白……这难道不是你想要的吗？"

"哦，是的，你总是知道我*想要*的是什么，对吧，蒯诗雷！"她尖锐地反驳道。

"哈？！？"

这两人像是围绕着彼此嘶吼、低语，背景的电视演播室迅速淡出。现在，只剩下两张脸，交替特写。

"或者说，你知道我根本*不想要*的东西，但你依旧*毫不在乎*！"

"！？！？"

"你怎么能假装这件事从未发生过？那一夜……在屋顶上？"

"黎美，对不起，你似乎很激动。我只是不明白你在说什么——"

Chapter 34: Dialogue

"Why can't you just leave me alone!?!?" the young girl yelled.

"What do you mean, Limei? I wanted to congratulate you...I mean it, it's so great! I just wish I'd been the one to do it first! Pearl Peony, oh well. But...I don't understand...Isn't this what you wanted?"

"Oh yes, you always know exactly what I *want*, don't you, Kuai Shilei!" she shrilly retorted.

"Huh?!?!"

These two were hissing and whispering around each other as the scenery of the TV studio quickly faded into the background. Now, it was just the two faces, in alternating close-ups.

"Or maybe you know exactly what I *don't want*, and you *still don't care*!"

"!?!?"

"How can you pretend this never happened? How you—that night—on the roof?"

"Limei, I'm sorry, you seem agitated. I just don't understand what you're saying—"

第三十五章: 神风特攻

她转身跑开。

他追了出去，走出门，步入明亮的正午阳光中。

如同一根矛，珍珠的阴影斜斜地投射在黑色停车场上。他轻柔却坚定地握住她的手臂。她呜咽着挣脱开来，视线被千万颗钻石模糊。

银色的车从左侧撞上了她

Chapter 35: Kamikaze

She turned and ran.

Chasing after her, he walked out the door and into the bright noon light.

Like a spear, the shadow of the Pearl was thrown diagonally across the black parking lot. He took her arm gently but forcefully. She sobbed and tore herself away. Her vision was blurred by one million diamonds.

The silver car hit her from the left, and lifeless Limei saw that the spotlight above her was the sun.

第三十六章:"救命,我怀孕了!"

之后,蒴诗雷会匆忙赶来并拨打急救电话。新闻编辑部的关切团队会涌出,围住这一引人注目的场景。当急救人员俯身查看她时,黎美只有三个字想说。她的嘴里,这三个字恰如其分地点击组合在一起,所有人都听到她清晰地念出它们。

Chapter 36: "Help, I'm Pregnant"

Later, Kuai would rush over and call an ambulance. Everyone appeared to surround this newsworthy scene. When the paramedics leaned down, Limei had only three words to say. Inside her mouth, they clicked into place, and everyone heard herself pronounce them perfectly.

EPILOGUE: AGAIN, AGAIN, AGAIN

~ Fourth Confucian Proverb ~

> "If language is not correct, then words do not correspond to the truth; if words do not correspond to the truth, then what must be done remains undone; if this remains undone, morals and art will deteriorate, and the people will stand about in helpless confusion."
>
> —Confucius

尾声: 再一次, 再一次, 再一次

~ 第四句孔子箴言 ~

> "名不正, 则言不顺; 言不顺, 则事不成; 事不成, 则礼乐不兴; 礼乐不兴, 则刑罚不中; 刑罚不中, 则民无所措手足。"
>
> —孔子

第三十七章：来自北京的电话

黎美在中联医院一个僻静的角落醒来，窗帘缝隙透进来的阳光洒在她身上。

在头部创伤病房外，耳边传来低声细语，时而清晰，时而模糊，就像缓缓眨动的眼睛。

"……她跑到马路上，好像指望我用手停下车一样…是的…在此之前她的表现很反常……"

"…我明白了。不，不…没有怀孕的迹象…可能有点混乱…头部受了伤…"

"天啊，我真是觉得很糟糕……我想我说了什么让她不开心的话，我一不小心就聊起了…我对她不太了解，但她是个好女孩…太敏感了…而我有时候会无意中说错话…"

但黎美并没有听到这些。她看到床边的电话闪烁着温暖的光。她一边接起电话，一边看着电视屏幕上自己的画面。几分钟后，黎美挂了电话。电话那头传来的声音是：

"你好，请问是黄黎美吗？我是吴子墨，导演……我想为一部大型历史战争剧物色女演员——《南京大屠杀》，你知道的——还有竹林，可能还有一些武打戏……我在新闻上看到了你事故的画面，真心为你感到遗憾，但那段视频确实很震撼……而且你最近的经历一定会让你的表演更加真实……等你恢复后，我希望能给你这个角色……是的……我会留我的电话号码……"

然后，她闭上眼睛，甜甜一笑，继续沉沉入睡。

Chapter 37: A Call from Beijing

Limei awoke to light shining through the blinds of a window in a secluded corner of SinoUnited Hospital.

Outside the head trauma ward, the voices that whispered faded in and out, in and out, like eyes blinking slowly.

"...ran into traffic, like she expected me to stop the car with my bare hands or something...yes...acting...right before..."

"...I see. No, no...signs of a pregnancy...may have been confused...a hit to the head..."

"God, I feel terrible...I think I said something to upset her, I got carried away...don't know her very well, but she's a...thin-skinned...and I can be insensitive..."

But Limei did not hear any of that. Instead, she saw the sunny song of the telephone by her bed. She picked up the phone while watching her scene on the TV screen. After several minutes, Limei hung up. This is what she heard:

"Hello, is this Huang Limei? This is Wu Zimo, yes, the director... I'm looking to cast an actress in a big historical wartime drama— Rape of Nanking, you know—bamboo groves and maybe some martial arts fighting as well...I've been watching the scene of your accident on the news, I'm so terribly sorry to hear of course, but it was really striking....And with this recent traumatic experience, I'm sure you'll be wonderful, so authentic...when you've recovered I'd love to offer you the part...yes... I'll leave my number..."

Then she closed her eyes, smiled sweetly, and slept.

鸡第三十八章: 或蛋？(田园景色)

晨曦明亮地洒在雪山之上,晨露柔和地映照在草地上。木桶里的牛奶闪耀着洁白的光芒。一颗桃子从高处静静坠落。

黎美对乡村风景甜美地微笑。

唱着一首简单的牧女之歌,她将自己倒退着送入了昏暗的鸡舍。

她回头望向天空,望向敞开的门,望向那已投在门槛上的阴影。然后,她向前看,望向金色的干草。

那里,空空的蛋壳如最纯净的珍珠般闪耀——而可爱的丽梅将它们收进了她的围裙。

Chapter 38: Chicken or Egg? (Pastoral Scene)

The dawn broke brightly over the snowy mountains. The dew shone softly on the morning grass. The milk flashed whitely in the wooden pail. A peach dropped, silent, from up on high.

Limei smiled sweetly at the country landscape.

Singing the song of a simple milkmaid, she turned herself backwards, into the darkened chicken coop.

She looked behind her, towards the sky, towards the open door, towards the shadow that had already been thrown across the threshold. She looked in front of her, towards the golden hay.

There, the empty eggs gleamed like purest pearls—and Lovely Limei gathered them in her apron.

待续....

第二部（抢先预览）

序章: 一个非常重要的人
一: 成为......一名演员?
二: 疯狂的酸涩
三: 玫瑰无论如何
四: 虞美人花的历史
五: 欲望
六: 镜头的眼睛
七: 符号的帝国
八: 历史课
九: 爱的坟墓
十: 桃花源
十一: 肥皂剧
十二: 合唱团
十三: 新女性
十四: 摄制组
十五: 你真不擅长这个, 是吗?
十六: 不要跌倒
十七: 天然捕食者
十八: 砰砰砰, 竹子
十九: 创造艺术, 而非战争
二十: 偶像
二十一: 服从
二十二: 世界末日......现在?
二十三: 她的最后一首歌
二十四: 开脸
二十五: 你敢咬我?
二十六: 剪, 剪, 剪!
二十七: 黑暗的心
二十八: 头部创伤
二十九: 我又感觉疯了 (再一次, 再一次, 再一次)
三十: 黑天鹅
三十一: 车祸
三十二: 格言
三十三: 阴影之林

To Be Continued....

BOOK II (Sneak Preview)

Prologue: A Very Important Person
1: Becoming....an Actress?
2: Wild Wild Sour
3: A Rose by Any Other Name
4: The History of the Iris
5: Desire
6: The Eye of the Camera
7: Empire of Signs
8: A History Lesson
9: Tomb of Love
10: Peach Blossom River
11: Soap Opera
12: Chorus
13: New Women
14: The Film Crew
15: You're Not Very Good at This, Are You?
16: Don't Fall
17: Natural Predator
18: Bam Bam Bam Bamboo
19: Make Art Not War
20: The Idol
21: OBEY
22: Apocalypse...Now?
23: Her Last Song
24: Face Opening
25: How Dare You Bite Me?
26: Cut, Cut, Cut!
27: Heart of Darkness
28: Head Trauma
29: I Feel Crazy (Again, Again, Again)
30: Black Swan
31: Car Crash
32: Aphorism
33: Grove of Shadows

注释

这本书最初是为了配合2022年在上海外滩美术馆举行的黛安·塞维林·阮(Diane Severin Nguyen)展览而委托创作的。展览以大约一个小时的视频《在她的时代》为中心，该视频的一个版本后来被纳入了2023年惠特尼双年展。这部电影的故事发生在浙江省横店市，这里是一个巨大的影视拍摄基地。影片讲述了一位名叫艾瑞斯（李美仙）的挣扎中的演员，为了首次主演一部以1937年南京大屠杀为背景的历史战争片所经历的旅程。随着艾瑞斯往返于她的公寓和横店的外景拍摄地，她在角色与现实之间来回穿梭：一会儿对着剧本练习台词，一会儿又面对镜头表演。随着阮的影片推进，虚构、历史与现实在再现中交织——成为一种用以构想未来的工具。

封面的黑白照片是阮玲玉的首部影片《爱与责任》(1931)的剧照；背面的照片则来自她的最后一部电影《新女性》(1935)；其余的封面和内页照片均来自《在她的时代》的剧照。这些拍立得照片是我在2022年8月上海拍摄的，当时黛安正在安装她的展览，而我正遭受脑震荡。

注释：我将《小粉书》构思为一种反常的误译：在黛安作品与我的创作之间；在媒体形式、语言与文化语境之间；也在关系之内。同时，它像一段展览文本或一册国家发行的宣传手册般，是一篇主题鲜明（甚至露骨？）的文字：《丽梅的生活》受制于多种概念和形式的约束，从类型化爱情故事的规范到德里达解构主义的教诲（这是一种个人癖好）；从屈辱的身份叙写作激励机制到我的东方主义幻想——"成为中国人"。当代文学将更抽象的美学尝试视为形式的滥用——丽梅便因此被大大"滥用"。

Note

This book was originally commissioned to accompany a 2022 exhibition by Diane Severin Nguyen at the Rockbund Museum in Shanghai. The exhibition centered on an approximately hour-long film, *In Her Time*, a version of which was later included in the 2023 Whitney Biennial. The film is set in Hengdian City, a massive movie-making complex in Zhejiang province, and follows the journey of a struggling actress named Iris (Li Meixian) as she prepares for her first leading role in a historical war film set during the 1937 Massacre of Nanjing. As Iris is shuttled back and forth from her apartment to the outdoor sets of Hengdian, she falls in and out of character: running lines one moment, addressing the camera the next. Over the course of Nguyen's film, fiction, history, and reality fuse into re-enactment—a tool for visualizing the future.

The black-and-white photo on the cover is a still from Ruan Lingyu's first film, *Love and Duty* (1931); the photo on the back, from her last, *New Women* (1935); the rest, as well as the front and end pages, are stills from *In Her Time*. The polaroids I took in Shanghai in August of 2022.

I conceived of *Little Pink Book* as a perverse mistranslation: between Diane's work and my own; between media forms, languages, and cultural contexts; and within relationships. At the same time, like a good exhibition text or a state-issued propaganda pamphlet, it is a thematically quite obvious (explicit?) text: the Life of Limei is fettered by a variety of conceptual and formal constraints ranging from the conventions of genre romance to the classroom theatrics of Derridean deconstruction (a personal fetish); the humiliating incentives to write from an "identity" position to, on the other hand, my Orientalist fantasy of "being Chinese." Contemporary literature considers more abstract aesthetic gestures an abuse of form—Limei, then, has indeed been much-abused.

延伸阅读

这篇文本可以被视为同人小说，也可以视为一种特别晦涩的艺术评论形式。韩炳哲的《山寨：中国式解构》为我在这两种体裁之间搭建了一座桥梁，他评论了中国绘画的历史传统，指出其中的作品不仅不断被其他艺术家修订，甚至还被"写上字"（确实如此）——最为珍贵的画作往往也被题写上书法行字。

2007年，互联网上访问量最高的博客属于中国电影明星徐静蕾。徐静蕾通过新浪微博分享她的日常生活：工作、饮食、她的想法和感受——但从NBC新闻的角度来看，她从未"提供过一系列的八卦故事"。
https://blog.sina.com.cn/u/1190363061.

中国拥有高度发达的网络文学文化。在过去十年中，许多最受欢迎的中国电视剧都是根据在晋江文学城 (jjwxc.net)，中国拥有高度发达的网络文学文化。在过去十年中，许多最受欢迎的中国电视剧都是根据在晋江文学城（

Further Reading

This text could be understood as either fanfiction or a particularly oblique form of art criticism. Byung-Chul Han's *Shanzhai: Deconstruction in Chinese* (2011) provided a link for me between these two genres via his commentary on the historical tradition of Chinese painting, in which works are not only continually revised by other artists, but written upon (literally)—the most highly-valued paintings also bear lines of calligraphy. In these multimedia artworks, an image appears literally within the same frame as the criticism and poetry inspired by it.

In 2007, the most visited blog on the internet belonged to Chinese movie star Xu Jinglei. Using microblogging platform Sina, Xu meditated on her daily life: work, diet, her thoughts and feelings—but never, in the words of NBC News, "providing a catalogue of kiss-and-tell stories."
https://blog.sina.com.cn/u/1190363061.

China boasts a highly developed culture of web-based literature. Many of the most popular Chinese TV dramas of the past decade were originally adapted from web novels published to sites like Jinjiang Literature City (jjwxc.net), where the vast majority of content is written by amateurs—almost exclusively women. These are often "coercive" romances. They also often involve time travel or metafictional conceits, like the protagonist falling into or out of a book or movie.

Bio

Diane Severin Nguyen (b. 1990) works with photography, video, and installation. Recent solo and group exhibitions include: The Whitney Biennial at the Whitney Museum of American Art, New York; SculptureCenter, New York; The Renaissance Society, Chicago; Rockbund Art Museum, Shanghai; Contemporary Arts Museum Houston; Contemporary Art Gallery, Vancouver; MoMA PS1, New York; Carnegie Museum of Art, Pittsburgh; Schinkel Pavilion, Berlin; Jeu du Paume, Paris; and Hammer Museum, Los Angeles. Her films have been screened at film festivals such as the New York Film Festival, International Film Festival Rotterdam, and Berlinale. Nguyen is a recent recipient of the 2023 Guggenheim Fellowship.

Chen S. is a professional translator on Fiverr. She has translated literature, instructional posters, exhibition texts, advertisement copy, invoices, a technical manual for Shanghai Yaohua Weighing System Co., and a French cookbook. She works between English, Russian, German, and Chinese.

Thank You

To Lucia Kan-Sperling, Alec Mapes-Frances, Pearl Silverman, and Signe Swanson for reading and editing. And to Vita Salvioni-Guttman, who had much advice about the sex scene.

To the Rockbund Art Museum, for first commissioning this project, and especially to Karen Wang, who was so helpful during my time in Shanghai.

To Diane Severin Nguyen, for everything!

MORE FROM ARCHWAY EDITIONS

Archways 1
 (edited by Chris Molnar and Nicodemus Nicoludis)
cokemachineglow: Writing Around Music 2005-2015
 (edited by Clayton Purdom)
Claire Donato – *Kind Mirrors, Ugly Ghosts*
John Farris – *Last Poems*
Gabriel Kruis – *Acid Virga*
Brantly Martin – *Highway B: Horrorfest*
NDA: An Autofiction Anthology
 (edited by Caitlin Forst)
Alice Notley – *Runes and Chords*
Ishmael Reed – *Life Among the Aryans*
Ishmael Reed – *The Haunting of Lin-Manuel Miranda*
Ishmael Reed – *The Slave Who Loved Caviar*
Mike Sacks – *Randy & Stinker Lets Loose*
Paul Schrader – *First Reformed*
Stacy Szymaszek – *Famous Hermits*
Erin Taylor – *Bimboland*
charles theonia – *Gay Heaven is a Dance Floor but I Can't Relax*
The Mystery of Perception
 (Lynne Tillman interviewed by Taylor Lewandowski)
Unpublishable
 (edited by Chris Molnar and Etan Nechin)
Lindsey Webb – *Plat*

FORTHCOMING

    Afsana Mousavi – *Love Story*
    Chris Molnar – *Heaven's Oblivion*
    Paul Schrader – *Hardcore*
    George Santayana - *The Sense of Beauty*

Archway Editions can be found at your local bookstore or ordered directly through Simon & Schuster.

Questions? Comments? Concerns? Send correspondence to:

    Archway Editions
    c/o powerHouse Books
    220 36th St., Building #2
    Brooklyn, NY 11232

OLIVIA KAN-SPERLING (b. 1997) lives in New York. Her first book, *Island Time* (Expat Press, 2021) about the psycho-geographies of Kendall Jenner and Lil Peep, is a recursive novella figured as a virtual world. It is accompanied by a vaporware product, *Music Video Guided Symbolization Reading Game*.